Donated by
Floyd Dickman

GINA.JAMIE.
FATHER.BEAR.

GINA.JAMIE. FATHER.BEAR.

GEORGE ELLA LYON

A Richard Jackson Book
Atheneum Books for Young Readers
New York · London · Toronto · Sydney · Singapore

In addition to those to whom this book is dedicated, the author wishes to thank the following people whose knowledge and insight helped bring it into being: Carol Bastian, Franny Billingsley, Marie Bradby, Jo Carson, Jan Cook, Martha Gehringer, Sharon George, Kathy Jo Gutgsell, Gladys Hoskins, Robert and Betty Hoskins, Diane James, Loyal Jones, Kate Kenah, Leatha Kendrick, Miyuki Lake, Ann Olson, Jenny Davis O'Neill, Kendra Marcus, Lou Martin, Graham Shelby, Ed Smith, Jimmy Stevens, Jacky Thomas, Roberta White, and Leah Winkler.

Atheneum Books for Young Readers
An imprint of Simon & Schuster Children's Publishing Division
1230 Avenue of the Americas
New York, New York 10020

Book design by Interrobang Design Studio

The text of this book is set in Bembo and Kaatskill.

Printed in the United States of America

First Edition

10 9 8 7 6 5 4 3 2 1

Library of Congress Cataloging-in-Publication Data

Lyon, George Ella, 1949-

Gina.Jamie.Father.Bear. / George Ella Lyon.

p. cm.

"A Richard Jackson book."

Summary: The lives of two young people, one in Ohio and one in another dimension, intersect as they struggle to hold their single-parent families together and to explain the behavioral changes they see in their fathers.

ISBN 0-689-84370-4

[1. Supernatural—Fiction. 2. Fathers—Fiction. 3. Secrets—Fiction. 4. Single-parent families—Fiction. 5. Family problems—Fiction. 6. Ohio—Fiction.] I. Title.

PZ7.L9954 Gi 2002

[Fic]—dc21   2001022991

for Dick,
who listened this book into being

for Steve,
guide and companion on the way

for Paula Raines
and the Monday night Dream Group

GINA.JAMIE.
FATHER.BEAR.

~ *BEFORE* ~

*H*alloween is just fake blood and costumes. The holiday that scares me is New Year's Eve, a door we all go through without a clue as to what's on the other side. I didn't always know this. Back in fourth grade, I thought New Year's was about fancy snacks and staying up late and having a friend sleep over so you could hang out the next day. That year it was Cristi Allen, my best friend in Shaker Heights.

We'd stayed up past midnight finishing a jigsaw puzzle, so we were slow starters on January first. But we'd had blueberry pancakes and Dad had lectured my big brother Mabry on the dangers of skating on the hardwood floor in his socks, when Mom said, "Would you girls like to make a New Year's necklace?"

"Out of what?" I asked, remembering the dumb macaroni ones we'd made in first grade.

Mom got a yellow plastic sack out of the pantry. BEAR-DANCE BEADS was printed on the side. "Out of these," she said.

Then she cleared off the white island in the white kitchen and poured bright beads from plastic bags into the bowls, set out strong thread, and put several sets of fasteners in a cup. "My New Year's resolution," Mom said, "is to make a necklace of the year."

"Just one?" Cristi asked.

"That's right," Mom told her. "I'll choose a bead a day. One of these for ordinary days"—she tilted the bowl of little beads, purple to blue—"and on a special day, I'll pick one of these." She held up a clear green bead with red dots on it, and an amber one like a teardrop.

"Cool," Cristi said.

"Special how?" I asked. "Like a birthday?"

"Sure," Mom said. "But also days that are special just for me. Days when I learned something."

"Like the day Mabry taught you to skateboard!" I said.

She laughed. "That might require two beads."

Just then Dad came in the kitchen. He had his topcoat on.

"I have to run by the Clinic, Meg," he said. "I should be back by supper." Then he noticed me and Cristi. "No holidays for a surgeon!" he declared, as if this was good news. He paused, seeing the beads. "Is this for Scouts?" he asked. Mom was one of the Scout leaders.

"Nope," I said. "It's for Mom. And us."

"She's making her life into a necklace," Cristi explained.

Mom took a deep breath. She looked at Dad, ran her fingers through her short brown hair, and went on talking to us. "If I keep the beads in the kitchen," Mom said, "they'll remind me to focus on the ingredients of my life, to remember I'm making something." She put one hand on Cristi's shoulder, the other one on mine. "But you girls don't need reminding. You can make a whole necklace today if you want."

She beamed. That's all you could call it. In her faded jeans and lilac sweatshirt that said "Plant dreaming deep," she looked like another kid.

"Interesting," Dad responded, though he looked b-o-r-d, as Mabry once said. "But I wouldn't do it here, Meg. This work surface is for food."

"Oh, I won't leave the beads here," she assured him. "I'll keep them on the desk." She gestured to the little cubby with a bulletin board over it right next to the refrigerator.

"That's for paying bills," Dad said.

"I know—" she started.

"And you can't pay them with beads," he cut in.

Cristi and I were looking from Mom to Dad to Mom as if this was a tennis match. There he stood all straight and neat and clipped and official, and there she was like a bird that's just landed and not arranged its feathers yet.

"I *know,* Martin," she said. "But—" Then, for some reason, she looked at me. "Oh, all right," she said, then shrugged, suddenly smaller. "I'll take the beads to the studio." She meant the three rooms nearby where she taught yoga.

"Good plan," he said. "Well, I've got to run. Have fun with your arts and crafts." As an afterthought, he added, "You probably *could* get a badge for jewelry-making, Gina. You should keep a record of this."

"Thanks, Dad," I said, and he was gone.

"What does a badge have to do with it?" Cristi asked.

Mom laughed. "What indeed?" she said. Then she showed us how to tie a fastener onto a thread and begin stringing the beads. Each of us could use five of the fancy beads, she said, and as many of the small ones as we needed. While we were getting started, she began her own necklace with a bead that looked like a dark purple crescent moon. Cristi and I had a blast making those necklaces, and after lunch we had more fun sledding with Mabry on Perth Hill. All in all it was a great New Year's Day.

If you don't count what I couldn't see then: that taking those beads to the studio was the first step of Mom's moving out. If she finished that necklace, she never wore it at home.

That spring, when Mabry was running track for the first time, Dad said he would take us to the meet. Mabry raised his eyebrows at me, and I shrugged. Dad had never done T-ball or soccer or Little League. He was always at work.

But that morning he drove us over to the field, dropped Mabry off at the coach's stand, and told me to find us a seat while he got hot chocolate and coffee. Spring is cold in Cleveland.

Halfway through the hurdles, as we huddled in the bleachers, I couldn't keep quiet any longer. "How come you're here?" I said to Dad.

"Am I not doing it right?" he asked.

"Doing what right?"

"Taking the kids to Saturday sports," he said.

"Dad, it's not like there are rules."

He laughed. "I know. But your mother always does this sort of thing. And she thinks I should . . ."

"You're doing great, Dad," I said, and leaned into his shoulder. His black wool coat was soft and held that sharp hospital smell. Around us, other dads had on sweatshirts and down jackets. But mine was headed to work when this was over. He had to make rounds at the Clinic.

The loudspeaker voice—which was really Mrs. McGinley, the coach's wife—announced: "And now, in the one-mile race, representing the seventh grade at Shaker Heights Junior High, number seven, Mabry Ourisman."

Mabry loped to the starting line, did his stretch, and took his stance.

"Do we cheer?" Dad asked.

"Sure," I said. "If you want to."

So when the flag went down, he stood up stiffly, hands at his sides, and yelled, "Go, Mabry!"

Mabe came in third. Telling Mom about it at dinner that night, he said, "Dad threw me off, yelling. I thought I was in trouble."

"I was cheering," Dad corrected. "Not yelling."

"I'm proud of you both," Mom said. "For trying new things." But she only looked at Mabry, that adoring-mother look.

"Yeah, going around in circles is hard," I said.

"What do you know about it, Punk?" he asked, and kicked me under the table.

"Stopping is harder," Mom put in.

"Not if you do it right," Mabry told her. "Coach says to power down but run it out. Stopping cold can cause cramps and do damage."

"I see," Mom said.

Did she look at Dad then to see if he saw, too? Or did she even hear Mabry's words that night the way I hear them now?

~ 1 ~

❀

*T*he sound of a car door slamming woke me up. I looked at the clock: 5:50. I had set it for 6:00, hoping to catch Dad, but he was already gone.

I jumped out of bed and ran downstairs. At least Mabry would be there. At least the house wouldn't be empty. Lights filled the kitchen, but no Mabe. Dad's cereal bowl was in the sink, the newspaper neatly folded, everything clear. That meant Mabry had not been there. He leaves a trail.

Then I heard the shower upstairs. Good. He was just getting up. It wasn't even 6:00 yet, and school didn't start till 7:50, so I could make us some breakfast and we could talk. I would make French toast, which he loves. I got out eggs, milk, butter, bread. Vermont maple syrup. I found some bacon-in-the-box that you zap in the microwave. Found the griddle. Mabry would like this.

Mom left us two years ago. Now I'm a freshman and Mabe's a senior, and he seems to be done with family. He's got his eye on something else. Dad does too.

Whisking milk into the egg, I saw how yellow and white blended together. Just the opposite of us. We used to be in the same bowl, headed in the same direction, but now it was like we were all separating, going back into the shells, the carton. Dad was gone all the time. True, he is a doctor, but he's *always* been a doctor. He didn't disappear before daylight when Mom was here. He didn't look right through you in the middle of a conversation or shut himself up in his study the minute supper was over and stay there all night. He didn't forget Parents' Night at school. Actually, he didn't forget that; he just tried to go the night after. . . . Was this depression? Was he seeing somebody else? If so, why at the crack of dawn? And why couldn't we meet her?

I thought about this as I melted the butter and dipped the bread and laid it on the griddle to sizzle and brown. Maybe if I could talk to Mabry, he could talk to Dad, sort of man-to-man. Dad thought I was still a kid, but Mabe would be going to college next year. He was almost grown.

I got out the place mats—one navy trimmed in yellow, one yellow and slate blue. They looked like flags on the white table, like semaphores. Dad used to take us sailing, back when he took off weekends, back when Mom was here, I thought, when we were a . . . but I stopped myself. We were still a family. We had to be. Early light was coming through the bay window of the breakfast nook, and everything looked new, hopeful.

Mabry bounded down the stairs and shot through the door just as I was pouring the orange juice. He had on sweats instead of his school clothes. "Gina!" he exclaimed. "You're supposed to be asleep!"

Six feet tall to my five feet five, Mabry towered over me, but back when we were small, with our yellow-white hair and pale eyes, people used to think we were twins.

"I woke up," I said. "I made us some breakfast."

"Nice," he said, glancing at the table. "But I can't eat. I've got to get to the track."

"It's soccer season," I said. "You don't have to run track." There was a little whine in my voice, which I hated.

"I need the extra work to get back in shape," he said.

School had only been in session a couple of weeks, but the truth was Mabry had run all summer, every day after his job at the book warehouse. He's never out of shape.

"So what are you going to eat?" I asked.

He opened the refrigerator, bent down, peered in. "I'll take these for later," he said, grabbing some yogurt and a PowerBar. "You can catch the bus?"

"Sure," I said. Mabry has this great falling-apart Saab, and that first couple of weeks, I loved riding to school with him. "See you at lunch!" I called, but he was already out the door.

ONE

At night, he was our own Da. He stirred porridge or sometimes a stew on the fire. He baked ash cakes. He fed the three of us at the plank table: Anadel, Lily, and me, called Jamie. Afterward, he sent us outside to scrub in the starlit waters of the trough. Then he gathered us to him by the fire on the leaf-filled tick where we would sleep, and he sang till we grew dozey. Sweet words smoothed by the burr of his voice:

> *"An earthly nurse sits and sings,*
> *And aye, she sings by lily wean,*
> *And little ken I my bairn's father*
> *Far less the land where he dwells in."*

"How could she not know her own bairn's father?" Anadel or Lily would ask, interrupting.

"Hush, lass. The song will tell you. Listen now!" he whispered, and continued.

"I am a man upon the land,
I am a silkie on the sea,
And when I'm far and far frae land
My home it is in Sule Skerrie."

And if he sang the whole song through before sleep took us, if we saw the silkie come with gold to claim his child, then would Lily and Anadel be in tears, in need of Da's soothing, while I huddled under the covers until they grew quiet and I could ask: "You will be here in the morning, Da? Just this once? You will be here when we wake up?"

"Shhh, Jamie. Do not fret! There's a good lad. A hunter needs to be underway before daybreak, you know. And some cures can only be found in the dark. Do not worry. I have left you porridge—"

And true to his word, he always left food to break our fast. But I wanted to say good-bye to him in the morning, to behold him on both sides of the day. So one night I kept myself awake to catch him. I chewed bark and named stars; I put a small, sharp rock under my back and moved it when sleep threatened. The hours crawled. But the moment Da slipped out the door, I leapt up and followed.

He was not in the yard, so I started on the path into the woods. "Da!" I called, and began to run. "It's Jamie. Wait for me!" Far ahead, I saw a blur of white and then heard crashing through leaves and underbrush. Whatever it was, it had left the path. I stopped and rubbed my eyes. Da would not wear white in the woods or flee in such a fashion. I was shaking.

Thinking myself bedazed by sleeplessness, I turned back. Whatever I was following would have crossed the Tavy before I got there, and I could go no farther, for Da had set that stream as our boundary. That and the mountain that began at our back door. I knew that Bridestowe lay to the north, for 'twas where Da went to sell his cures, but I had never seen it. Whenever I asked, he said, "Someday. You'll see it when it is time." But I had seen twelve years come and go, and I was tired of answers that were not answers and lines that I could not cross.

My head was down, thinking on this, as I made my dawn-walk home, and so I noticed the tracks on the forest path, my own and those that should have been Da's. His were larger than you would think such as man would make. But then, they were not man-tracks. They were the deep, clawed tracks of a bear.

~ 2 ~

✳

I caught Mabry's eye across the cafeteria and motioned him over. He carried his orange tray with its plate of taco salad and glass of Mello Yello to my table. "Hey!" he said. "Why the welcome?"

"We've got to talk about Dad," I said as he slid into the plastic chair.

"Come on, Gina!" There was exasperation in his voice. "Don't start that again."

"Something's going on!" I insisted.

"Like what?" Mabry said, a forkful of lettuce, cheese, and seasoned meat poised before his mouth.

"I don't know," I told him, hearing the edge in my voice. "Ever since Mom left . . ."

Mabry's eyebrow shot up as his jaw chomped down.

"He leaves home before it's light and he goes somewhere—"

"He goes to work, Gina."

"Not just to work. The car has too many miles on it."

"My sister, the detective!" Mabry mocked. Half his lunch

was gone already. "He's a doctor, Gina. He has to keep long hours. And as for the mileage, maybe the Clinic's loaned him to another hospital. Give it a rest. You watch too much TV."

"That's not it!" I said, feeling tears tighten my throat. "You *know* something's wrong. He's acting weird at home, too."

"Well, maybe," Mabry conceded. "But if there is something, I think it's his business, and I don't want to get into it." He was pushing a lone shred of lettuce around with his last taco chip.

"Want this?" I asked, holding up my full plate.

"Sure!" he said, taking it from me. "You trying to lose weight or something?"

"No. I fixed a big breakfast. Remember?"

He nodded. "Still, if you're going to skip meals, be sure to keep your electrolytes in balance. Drink some Gatorade."

"Thank you, Almighty Athlete," I said, getting up. "I'm off to class."

"See you at home," he said between bites.

While it lasts, I thought.

TWO

Many days went by
before I could again follow Da, before the morning I set the water bucket on the table and said,
"Anadel, it's you have got to mind Lily today while I go into the
forest in search of cures."

"But Da does that," she said, her black hair in tangles from
sleep, her blue eyes dreamy. "Folks come to him—"

"I am older now," I boasted, "and I am learning."

Thinking to be gone all day, I put bread in a pouch at my waist
and set off.

It was a shiny morning, brim with birdcry. Still, my heart
shuddered as I followed this day's bear tracks, noting that their
stride was much longer than Da's. How big a beast was it? Did it
carry Da off every morning?

I followed the tracks to the stream. Everything on my path
until then said Stop. But at the water's edge, the tracks led me
forward. I took a breath and waded across but found no trail on
the other side. Who was this Bear, this creature who could come

out of the water but leave no track? I had to trail him without knowing.

Perhaps, I thought, Bear waded downstream to where the water pools and deepens to fish. So I did likewise. I found no bear, but the rainbow trout were darting.

Perhaps Bear climbed a tree, I thought, and even now looks down upon me. I scanned the branches of hickory and oak as I waded back to where I had entered. No Bear. No branch-broken sign of Bear.

Perhaps Bear is a night-hunter and has denned up somewhere, I thought. Perhaps he's snug in the rockhouse. Since nothing marked the ground, I would have to follow my mind's path. So I stepped out of the steam and followed the path far and far, up hill and down, till I came to the place where the Ash Tree grows.

Da has told us of this tree, which stands at the center of the forest, so tall that its branching begins at the height where our chimney ends. I stood for a moment with my hand on its ridged bark. That steadied me. Then I followed the path around and turned on a dimmer trace that I hoped led to the rockhouse. Da had said that it was just above the Ash Tree, and I thought Bear might have sheltered there. In steep zigzag through may-apple and cucumber I climbed Amicombe Hill.

Over half the day was gone when I reached the rockhouse, and I trembled as I stepped into the cool dark. What if Bear *was* there and I should wake him?

I had no torch to light the damp shadows. I saw no movement. "Bear?" I called. And, with harder heartbeat, "Da?"

No response. I sat myself down to eat of the bread I had brought. And easily after fell into a sleep.

Before me a woman stood, fair-haired like Lily. She smiled as if she knew me and took a ring from her finger. Holding it with both hands, she put it to her lips and kissed it, a golden O. Then she slid her hands apart and the ring grew larger—a bracelet, a barrel-hoop, a portal. Through it, I saw a bear and her cubs. One climbed on its mother's back; the other two tumbled under her as she walked. In the strangeness of sleep, I wanted to be with them, and I moved closer. The woman shook her head. Still, a longing drew me, and as I tried to step through the ring, she lifted her hand. A force, a solidity of air, barred my way. Not for me, that world. But I was given something. Turning away, I saw words written inside the circle. And though I do not know letters' speech, a voice sang:

One tree Many branches In the hollow Bear dances

And then I woke, blinking my eyes slowly as the world outside the rockhouse reappeared. For shame, Jamie, I thought, wasting day-light in foolish dreams! My head ached with questions that I could not stay to ponder. Fading light bid me run to beat Da home.

~ 3 ~

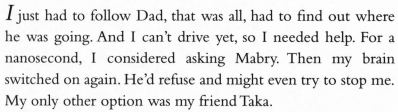

I just had to follow Dad, that was all, had to find out where he was going. And I can't drive yet, so I needed help. For a nanosecond, I considered asking Mabry. Then my brain switched on again. He'd refuse and might even try to stop me. My only other option was my friend Taka.

She's a junior, so this is the first year we've been in school together, but I've known her a long time. She was Mom's yoga student, and since my elementary school was close to the studio, I would walk there on the days Mom taught after-school classes.

Taka was about twelve when she first showed up and had been in America four years. Very serious. Also very stiff. I remember Mom telling her, "Relax, Taka. Let the movement flow, like music." Mom wanted everything to flow, and Dad wanted it to stay put. . . .

Anyway, Taka's mom tutors Japanese, and her father teaches math at Case Western, the university downtown, so Mom usually gave Taka a ride home after class. We got to know each other just hanging out while Mom closed up shop.

Taka was a little shy, but I was only ten and full of questions, like did she eat rice for breakfast and were chopsticks the same sticks Japanese women used in their hair. (I got this idea from my geisha doll.) Taka laughed. And she has a great laugh, like glitter spilling. So we became friends.

After Mom left, I didn't see Taka much, but she called sometimes. Since she plays violin and I play viola, we'd meet at Suzuki stuff. Now that I'm in high school, we're in orchestra together and I see her every day. Kind of a reunion. She has a car and offered to give me a ride home from afterschool practices.

So at the end of orchestra one day, I told her my worries about Dad and asked if she'd consider going for a longer ride.

"How long?" she asked. I could hardly hear her over the clatter of chairs scooting and instruments being put up.

"I don't know. I don't know where Dad's going. That's the point."

"But he goes early?" she asked, turning the knob to loosen her bow.

"Before light."

"So we might not miss any school."

"Might not," I told her.

"My mom would panic if the office called and said I hadn't shown up," she said.

"Well, we could turn around if it got that late," I offered.

She was settling the bow into its gold velvet case. "I don't think they call till second hour, anyway," she said.

That meant she would do it. "Yes!" I said.

"But you'll need to sleep over at my house the night before."

That made sense. And it was an adventure in itself. I'd *been* to Taka's once with Mom for tea, but that was all. She lives in a big house with almost no furniture. You leave your shoes at the door. You eat sitting on a pillow at a low table, across from a huge painting of birds. Taka says they're cranes. Even Nikko, her terror of a little brother, is quiet in that house. There's always incense on a small table in the front hall and flowers by the window.

Taka told her mom that we were going to an early yoga class and that I needed to stay over because Dad couldn't take me. Since Mom had driven Taka home all those times, Mrs. Yamamoto was glad to let Taka return the favor.

Unlike her daughter, who is tall and has that presence that yoga people get, Mrs. Yamamoto is short and small and sort of wavery. Her clothes aren't Japanese, but they aren't quite regular, either, and she bows and backs away a lot. Taka says she's just shy.

But she acted really glad to see me. "Gina!" she exclaimed when I got there. "So glad! So good!"

And our dinner was fancy: rice wrapped in seaweed, different-colored pickled things, and some kind of fish stir-fried with lots of ginger. When I said how much I liked it, Nikko said, "I'll bet at your house you have macaroni and cheese."

His mother shushed him. "You sure you like, Gina?" she asked, her dark eyes bright.

"Yes, thank you," I said, though the fish was a little tricky to swallow. "It's delicious."

At the head of the table, Mr. Yamamoto beamed. I could tell that having company was an event.

"Or nachos," Nikko insisted.

"You must like cheese," I told him.

"I like all American stuff," he said.

"We have American stuff too," Taka put in. "This is for company."

Mr. Yamamoto cleared his throat.

Taka says her family doesn't think like Americans. They wouldn't have let her have a car if it weren't for her music. With her dad at work and her mom tutoring, it got harder and harder for Taka to get to the groups and workshops that advanced students go to. So the car is for *music,* Mrs. Yamamoto says. "Is not for run-around-do-everything." Yoga is okay, though. And doing something before school means you're working hard.

So we crept out at 5:00 and parked around the block from my house. Taka had made us a thermos of Lapsang souchong, and the car was filled with its dark peach smell.

The longer we sat there, the more nervous I got.

"What's wrong with your finger?" Taka asked.

"What?"

"You keep pulling on it."

I looked down at my hands. "I'm trying to get this ring

off," I told her. "It's been stuck since I broke my finger."

Taka shook her head. "Viola players shouldn't break their fingers."

"I know. I was pitching for Mabry without a glove."

"Smart!" she said, then touched the gold band carved with leaves. "It's pretty. Is it a wedding ring?"

"I don't know. There's writing in it, but it's too small to read. Mom gave it to me when she left."

Just then, at 5:45, Dad's Sable turned the corner—the corner opposite from his usual route to work. "Ah-ha," I said. "Follow that car!"

I was clowning like an old-movie character, but I felt like a creep. Also, as we threaded through two lanes of traffic, then four, then six, I was praying not to lose him and equally scared of finding him. We were way past the suburbs, into downtown Cleveland, then onto the freeway, and I had *no idea* where he was headed. Not to a hospital—he passed them all. Not to any clinic that I'd ever heard him mention. It was 7:00 when he pulled in at a McDonald's on the far side of Akron.

We waited in the parking lot, in a space six cars away from his. Both of us wanted food and needed a bathroom, but we were afraid of being discovered. Anyway, he wasn't in there long. In less than ten minutes he came out with a large sack, a cardboard caddy with two cups in it, and a woman. A little stoop-shouldered, she wore the ugly green McDonald's shirt, black pants, and white nurse's shoes. And she had this geyser of curly red hair.

THREE

LIGHT WAS BUT THREE ROSE
LINES IN THE SKY WHEN HOME CAME INTO VIEW. SUNSET
SOFTENED THE STONE FACE OF THE COTTAGE, STONE DA
had carted up from the creek. He had built it not only strong and
safe, but lovely, with the moon and stars carved above the door. I
stepped inside.

"Da?" Anadel called. Her back was to me as she stirred something on the fire.

Lily laughed. "Not Da! 'Tis Jamie, and all red-faced and out of
breath he is."

"Aye," I said.

"And did you find the feverfew you went in search of?"

God alive! That purpose fled once I had put my foot to the
path!

"No," I spluttered. "I searched high and low and found none."
The searching part was true, and it steadied my heart a little.

"You're a funny boy, Jamie," Lily said, a teasing lilt in her voice. "Isn't he, Ana? Isn't our Jamie a funny one?"

"Daft, more like," Ana said as she squatted to stir the ashes. "Fetch us some water, then, Jamie. If you can't find that, you are witched."

Witched! The word stung like nettles. I grabbed the bucket from the shelf and rushed outside, as if I could escape it, as if closing the cottage door, I could shut out the bear tracks and the woman and the words singing in the ring. 'Twas a dream, I told myself. Nothing more! Yet still my heart was at a gallop. Still, my eyes were so full of that sight that I almost collided with Da.

I stumbled, and he caught my shoulders. "Jamie," he said, his voice concerned but easy. "Is the house afire?"

"No, Da, though I am after water."

"Mind your path, then."

"But, Da—"

"Yes, Jamie?"

"I need to learn about cures and such. You need to take me with you in the woods, and teach me what you know."

He stepped away a little. He saw I saw. "I was thinking soon to show that to your sisters," he said.

"But *you* do it, Da. And you can teach me more about hunting at the same time. I could tend the snares on the other side of the stream."

"You're a sprouting lad," he said, patting my head. But his smile did not hide the trouble in his voice. "I will think on it. Perhaps some night soon . . ."

"Night, Da? Will we not need light?"

"There's many an herb can only be plucked by the moon," he told me.

"I see," I said. But I did not say what I saw. Nor did I weep a child's tears. I must be strong, shouldering this secret. I must stand tall to face what was taking our Da.

~ 4 ~

✳

"*W*ho's *she?*" Taka asked.

"I have no idea."

"Really?" Taka's voice rose in amazement.

I nodded.

"Wow!" she said.

Dad turned left out of McDonald's onto a very busy road. There were three cars between us before we got out of the parking lot. Then traffic lights held us up. Anyway, for half an hour we drove the way we thought he was headed, but finally admitted we had lost him. We were back at the McDonald's by eight forty-five.

An old lady waited on us. I mean old. I don't think grandmothers should have to shovel French fries. She looked tired at the start of the day. ROBYN, her gold plastic pin read. There were lots of service tokens on her hat. "May I help you girls?" she asked.

We gave her our orders, and when she brought the drinks, I said, "You know the red-haired lady who works here?"

"Esther?" she asked.

"The one with all the hair," Taka added.

"Yes," Robyn said.

"Umm . . ." I wasn't sure what to say next. Finally I blurted, "Where does she live?"

"Heavens! *I* don't know," Robyn said. "Is she a friend of yours?"

I shook my head.

"Do you want to talk to the manager?"

"Oh, no," I said. I hadn't seen this coming. "Thanks. We'll catch her later."

Taka giggled. Robyn got our sausage biscuits.

Back in the car, Taka said, "What was that supposed to mean?"

"What?" I asked, between bites. The bad-for-you-breakfast tasted *so* good.

"Saying you'll *catch* Esther later."

"Oh. It didn't sound weird, did it?"

"Only to me," Taka said.

"I just freaked out when she said that about the manager. He'd tell Esther we were looking for her for sure."

"Robyn might too," Taka pointed out.

"I guess so," I agreed. We were back on the road now. "Hey! Remember that mall we passed? We could spend the morning there and still get home by dismissal time."

"Not a chance," Taka said. "I've got to get back to school."

"Oh, come on! Live a little!" I urged her.

She took one hand off the steering wheel, twisted her long

dark hair together and lifted it away from her neck. "I mean to live a lot," she said. "That's why I don't want to do anything dumb. Besides, you'll be wanting to go on this wild dad chase again, right?"

"Sure," I said. "Tomorrow."

"No, no. Not tomorrow! We can't both be absent two days running. We've got to do this so we don't get caught."

"All right," I said, resigned to having to face another lecture on the classification system in biology. "At least I will have missed English."

"*And* first hour," Taka reminded me. "What do you have then?"

"Study hall," I told her. "That's when I do my Spanish."

Taka laughed. We were roaring up the ramp onto I-77 now, and the little car was straining like our lawn mower right before it died.

A double semi with the words BEULAH LAND in red letters on its side almost didn't let us merge, but Taka kept up the speed, and he moved over.

"Go, girl!" I said, and polished off the last crisp bite of hash browns.

FOUR

I HAD TO ASK DA THREE
MORE TIMES BEFORE HE TOOK ME WITH HIM. "WE MUST
WAIT FOR A FULL MOON," HE TOLD ME. FINALLY, IT CAME.
Da went ahead of me down the path, the pack basket with the
leather strap over his shoulder. As we crossed the Tavy, he said,
"This you must never do without me."

"I know, Da." I did not like lying. Nor having to pretend I had
never been on this path.

We must have walked almost an hour before Da stopped to
dig. He showed me the spotted leaf-blades of lungwort. "For
anything that ails the breathing," he said. Then he dug gener-
ously around it, securing a clump of roots as big as the plant. This
he placed in the basket.

"All we need is here, Jamie," Da told me as we walked on.
"Here in the forest for the finding, if we but know it. So you
must memorize each leaf-shape and where it grows, each berry or
root and what it is good for.

"Everything has its match, its balance. That is how I was taught. So if you need tonic or salve, this yellow dock is what you seek." Da knelt and pointed out the plant with his knife. "Its flowering is long past, but the root is still strong, and 'tis the root you are wanting. . . ."

After that he found feverfew, slippery elm bark, and hawthorn berries. I tried to pay attention to all his instructions and explanations, but kept wanting to cry out, Da, can you not see I've come to learn something else?

When the night was half gone, we reached the Ash Tree, so tall in the dark, its branches seemed to be the bones of heaven. Da pointed out another tree, a Yew, which grew nearby. "Some say that tree is hollow and has a great room inside, but I have never found the door." He had broken off teaberry leaves for us to chew, and handed me some. They gave a sweet flavor to the air.

We sat in silence. I tried to pry words whole from my heart the way Da dug for the rootball, so they might thrive. When I thought I had lifted them free, I began, "Da?"

In the dark, he started. And the jerk of his limbs, the shock of his sleeping when I was wildly awake, caused me to drop my words.

"Yes, Jamie?" His voice sounded deep and hollow, hauled up as it was from the well of sleep.

I scrambled for more words, tore them loose, like a raccoon scavenges a garden. "I want to know where you go. It is not these woods, is it, Da? Because I have—"

"Jamie!" He was bolt awake now, angry. "You are not to be following me or planting questions like thorns in my path! I go where I have to go to keep you and Anadel and Lily fed and safe. There are things you must not ask!"

"But, Da—"

"'Tis a witching world, lad. And there are powers we must not play with. Do you understand?"

"But when I am a man—"

"Please God you live to be a man!" Da exclaimed. "By then you will be gone from here. Town will take you—and your sisters too."

"But why?"

"It must!" he said fiercely. And then, "It is better that way. You will learn a trade: hostler, cooper, blacksmith. And your sisters will marry. Until such time I will teach you all I can of hunting and of herbs. But study no farther, lad, as you love your life."

With that, he rose and bid me follow him back the way we had come.

*M*abry had soccer after school, so I didn't get to tell him what Taka and I had seen till supper was over. It was my night to clean up the kitchen, and that delayed me, too. Dad had fixed salmon, and the broiler pan was a mess. The house reeked. How can something smell so good when you're hungry and so rotten when you're not?

About 7:15 I knocked on Mabry's door. "Hey, Mabe! Are you in there?"

"No," he called back.

"Want to go for a walk?"

"No," he said again.

"Can I come in?"

"Okay, but make it quick. I've got to get through this calculus so I can start my lab report."

I was in Mabry's room by then, a maze of model everything: airplanes, insects, some kind of engine, a city center project he'd done for Art and Design. Mabry, the future engineer.

"I followed Dad today," I said, scooting Mabe's gym bag over so I could sit on the bed.

"Gina!" He turned around from the desk. "Of all the stupid—"

"No, listen! Taka and I got up very early and trailed him, and you know where he went?"

"The Clinic?"

I shook my head.

"Mount Sinai?"

"Nope."

"Lakeside?"

"Huh-uh."

"St. Vincent's?"

"*None* of these, Mabry. He didn't go to a hospital."

"Who is this Taka person, anyway?"

"You know Taka. She's first violin in orchestra."

"You mean Taka Yamamoto?"

"*Mabry*—"

"Isn't she a junior?"

"Don't you want to hear about Dad? He went to a McDonald's in Akron and picked up a woman with red hair."

"*He did what?!*" Mabry leaped up like the desk chair was on fire.

"Lots of red hair. And her name is Esther."

"You're sure?"

I nodded.

"You are *sure* it was Dad?" He leaned toward me, his blue eyes blazing.

"I'm not blind, Mabry. I know my own father!"

"All right, all right. So then what happened?"

"They drove off and we tried to follow, but we lost them in all the traffic."

His room being too crowded to pace, Mabry sat down. "Way to go, Dad!" he said.

"I told you something was going on," I said sounding satisfied, which was not how I felt.

He took a deep breath. "I think you should forget this," he said.

"What?" It was my turn to jump up.

"Dad's business is Dad's business. I'm forgetting it already."

"Mabry!" I wanted to punch him. Or take him by those broad shoulders and shake him till he woke up. "Don't you care—"

"Would you want Dad spying on *you?*" he interrupted. Then he took a deep breath and changed tactics. "And what if it was Dad, but he was in a parallel universe?"

"Yeah, right, Mabry."

"Really. We studied this last year. Time isn't a line, like we think. It's more like—"

"Mabry!" He came out of it. "I wasn't in a parallel universe. I was in Akron."

He laughed.

"It's not funny. Dad was with—"

"Never mind who he was with. He's divorced. He can see whoever he wants to."

"This wasn't like that," I insisted. "They weren't going out."

"How do you know?"

How *did* I know? "He didn't touch her," I said.

Mabry put his hands over his ears. "I don't want to hear about it! I want you to *leave this alone.* You're not the only one involved here, Gina. You get everything in an uproar and we'll all pay for it. Let it rest for a year, can't you? You and Taka just focus on your music till I'm gone."

I looked at him. I wanted to say, What about Dad? The family? And what about *me?* But Mabry found words before I did. "I mean it, Gina," he said. "Just let it go."

FIVE

"You are not to be fol-
lowing me," Da had said. "Study no farther, as
you love your life."

It was loving my life that kept me bound, that all the long summer and fall did not let me cross the stream again alone. Then the
world turned upside down. We woke one morning to hard winter with leaves still on the trees. Lily thought the piled snow and
piercing air a lark, but Ana and I knew we were in danger. We
had not gathered all the winter wood. And Da could not help.
Days grew shorter, and he was gone part of nighttime, too.

For a week we searched near home for any scrap of wood not
wet or frozen. Then the weather worsened. Deep in the whitest
days, when bitter winds and needle-ice kept us in—though not
Da! Da went!—we had barely enough heat to keep blood moving. So I crossed the stream for fire.

I crossed and was looking for treefall. Sometimes if you chop
through the snow-crust covering one, you will find, near the
crown, dry branches between the trunk and what rests on the

ground. Tricky it is to get at the underside and to sever these limbs without the giant coming down on you. It needs a sharp axe, strong arm, and quick eye. These I had. And a family growing cold.

So I leapt and slid across the white, hard stream. Snow was above my knees on the other side, but there was a trough-path made by Da or Bear, and I scrambled into it. Even following this was difficult. The tools were heavy and I was soon hot, my throat raw with cold. But I kept on.

I had not gone far beyond the Tavy I saw off to the left a huge oblong tomb of tree. I waded over and with my shovel cleared a space to work. By the time I had cut through the snow-and-ice mantle of the tree, my whole body steamed. I took off Da's old jacket, a full coat for me, and hung it on a branch stub. The tree was hickory and, sure enough, it had been down long enough and the branches were full enough that I could find a dry layer. I cut for a time, filling up the pack basket and the canvas sledge I would drag behind.

When I had finished and was putting on the jacket again, it struck me: Da would see this work. There was no way he could miss the journey and return, my labor written in the snow.

And my heart, already speeded up, lunged with fear. "No farther," I heard him say again. I looked up into ice-bright branches: everything brittle, everything ready to break. "No farther, as you love . . ." And I might have sunk into that snow, let myself drift into its pillows, if there had not blazed before me in all that white a window, the golden ring from the rockhouse. Through it, I saw Anadel's face, pale beneath her soot-black hair. "Jamie! Come home!" she wailed. "It's a bear!"

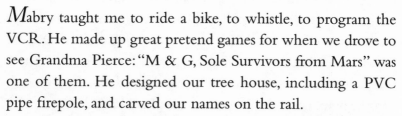

~ 6 ~

Mabry taught me to ride a bike, to whistle, to program the VCR. He made up great pretend games for when we drove to see Grandma Pierce: "M & G, Sole Survivors from Mars" was one of them. He designed our tree house, including a PVC pipe firepole, and carved our names on the rail.

In fact, he was the world's best big brother till Mom said she was leaving, till the word came down like a cosmic axe and split everything apart.

It wouldn't have been so bad if Mom had stayed single and moved to Cleveland Heights, or at least somewhere we could go on weekend visits, but no, she waited three months and married Whit the baker and moved to North Carolina, his home territory. We go there twice a year, sometime during Christmas break and sometime over the summer.

It's never just a visit, though. Oh, no. Whit says it's "an integrative family time." This means we *work* together (and I accidentally put flour instead of powdered milk in the quiche mix in the bakery at 4 A.M.), we *play* together (freezing our bones in a pool fed by mountain springs), and we *hike* together. Hiking is the best, because we do see neat stuff sometimes. But it's also the worst. It takes forever. Like last time, right before school started.

"How much farther?" I asked, leaning into the steep path, huffing under the weight of jeans and hiking boots and a day-pack of food and water.

And from the front of the line, Whit proclaimed, "Just till we get there. You'll hear it before you see it."

"I *hate* this," I muttered to Mabry, who was right in front of me.

"Don't whine," he hissed.

"I'm not whining!" I said, disgusted. "We've been in these woods for hours, and I just want to know how far to the stupid waterfall."

As if on cue, Whit declared, "You're going to love it."

Oh, right, I thought. That's what Mom told us about you.

"Are you okay, Gina?" This was my mother, who was last in our staggering line. Marissa, Whit's eight-year-old, was in between us.

Before I could answer, Mabry put in, "What about me? I've given my skin to maintain the insect population."

"I want to see!" Marissa cried in her high little voice. She's always afraid she'll be left out.

"He's kidding, Tadpole," Whit told her, his voice pitched below the crunch of sticks and leaves.

So I never answered Mom's question about being okay.

Did she really want to know? I wondered. If she cared, would she have left us? Would she have married this Happy Hiker and taken off? But it was too hot—yes, it's hot in the woods in August, I don't care how far up you are—and I was too sweaty and itchy to keep wondering. I trudged on. At least I still had my world.

Well, that world minus Mom.

The path turned, and I could hear the rushing water.

"Man, I'd like to be in that," Mabry said.

Whit topped the rise in front of us. "There it is!" he sang out.

Mabry sprinted the rest of the way. "Cool," he said.

I didn't hurry. Water is water. But, well, okay, when I got there this *was* something. It had two drop-offs, like giant steps that the water poured down, and the air in between was white with spray.

"Great Bear Falls," Whit said. "Or, as folks here say, Big Dipper and Little Dipper."

Sometimes Whit included himself in "folks here," though Mom said he'd lived away from these mountains as long as he'd spent growing up in them.

He went on, "Not so long ago, when the First People lived here"—(Whit meant Indians. That's the way he talks.)— "they knew that Spirit connects all things—"

I made my hand like a telephone and held it away from my ear to show Mabry how bored I was, but he was looking at Whit, listening. Sheesh!

"And they knew that the bears they hunted, bears who

themselves hunted in these woods and fished in these waters, were related to the Great Bear in the Sky."

"The Big Dipper!" Mabry said, excited. This is why teachers love him.

"Yes!" Whit said. "So our names for the falls came from that vision."

"Daddy," Marissa broke in, "you mean Indians lived on this mountain?"

"They sure did."

"How do you know?"

If I'd asked a question that way, Dad would have told me not to be a smart aleck, but Whit just said, "Well, honey, wherever people live, they leave things behind, like tools and weapons and pottery, and other folks find them."

"And bones," Mabry added.

"You mean dead people?" Marissa asked. Her little eyebrows and her whole face squinched up. She was that interested.

"Yes. Human bones and animal bones, too," her daddy told her. "From the creatures they hunted."

"Like bears," Mabry said.

"We are thinking!" Whit said, too happy. He has this "we" thing, always trying to turn Mabry and me into his family. But you can't make a family like you make an army. You can't just draft kids. And anyway, we had a family until he came along.

"So bears would be in the water and Indians would shoot them dead," Marissa declared, crouching down at the edge of the stream and pulling back an invisible string on her invisible bow.

"No, no," Whit said, earnest again. "The First People didn't hunt bears like that. They waited till spring for someone to dream where a bear's den was—you know bears sleep through the winter. Then a hunting party would go to that spot and call the bear, saying, 'Grandfather, come out!' and then—"

Whit didn't notice that his daughter had quit listening. She was pulling on Mom's arm.

"Whit," Mom interrupted, "that's fascinating, but these kids are hungry. Why don't we put out our picnic and eat while we listen?"

"All right," Whit said, looking confused. He took a blue tarp from his pack and spread it on the least slopey bit of ground near the falls. I was just about to sit down when he commanded, "Tick check!" and we had to line up for the once-over.

Then we sat down to assorted sandwiches made at the bakery: cream cheese, olive, and nut (yuk!); soybean and herb spread (double yuk!); and turkey and havarti (the ones in my pack). As I handed some to Mom, she looked at my hand. "You're still wearing Mother's ring," she said.

"Um-hmm," I said. Like it meant anything.

"I've always wondered where it came from," she said, taking out a plastic bag of carrot and celery sticks and sliding it across the tarp to Whit.

"You told me it was Grandma Pierce's," I said.

"That's right, Gina!" Mom looked so pleased that it made me sad and mad at once. She'd given me the ring as a birthday present right after she and Dad split up. I didn't want it then or now, and I didn't want to be remembering. "It was Mother's wedding ring," Mom continued. "But my father had found it in a pawn shop somewhere. They were too poor to afford a new ring—"

Mabry broke in. "She just wears that ring because she can't get it off," he said. "She was pitching for me bare-handed. I hit a pop fly and she caught the ball. Broke her finger."

Go, Mabe, I thought. Mom looked away.

Later, on the flight home, Mabry pointed out that the woods make Whit lecture more and they make Mom sappy. "Sappy," he said, hooting. "It's a pun. Get it?"

Half the time he doesn't think I'm conscious. The other half he wishes I wasn't. I tell Taka this when I tell her about Mabry's ban on following Dad.

"Dumb jock!" she said.

"Whoa," I told her, laughing. "He's supersmart."

"I mean dumb in the heart," she said.

We waited two weeks before we followed Dad again, and all he did was go to St. Vincent's downtown. We were at school before the first bell.

Then we had to wait two more weeks because Taka said her mother was going to get suspicious about crack-of-dawn yoga classes if they came too often. As it was, she just said, "You girls have much dedication."

It was a foggy morning—we get a lot of fog off the lake—
and Taka didn't like driving in it. She'd only had her license a
few months and did not enjoy "hurtling blindly through
space," as she put it.

But the fog lifted, the sun climbed as we drove south, and
pretty soon it was fun whizzing past bright maples, heading
for a new place. Is this what Dad feels? I wondered. Is it all
about escape?

Taka and I had a plan this time. Assuming Dad went to the
same McDonald's, we'd pull in at the gas station across the
street. Then when he pulled out, we'd slip into traffic one car
behind them.

It would have worked, too, I think, but Dad sped right past
McDonald's and clear out of Akron, and turned on the road
to Cuyahoga Falls. About twenty minutes into tawny fields
dotted with more blazing trees, he put on his left turn signal.

"Slow down," I told Taka. "Don't get too close. And when
he turns, keep going."

Taka drove on far enough to make our return inconspicu-
ous, then turned around.

I had been afraid Dad might notice us after we got on the
two-lane road, because all the traffic evaporated and we
couldn't keep a buffer car between us. But I don't think he
ever looked back. This made me feel bad. I know it's crazy, I
know I didn't want to get caught, but it made me feel like
he'd forgotten his family, his *life,* almost like I didn't exist. I
said this to Taka as we were backing out of a gravel drive, and
she reached over and pinched me.

"Ow!" I said. "What's that for?"

"You're real," she said, and started to laugh.

"Don't make me laugh!" I cautioned. "I've got to pee."

"Ah," she intoned, in her fake Asian-in-American-movie voice, "you feel pinch. You feel pee. You real."

Before we stopped at the mailbox where Dad had turned, we scanned the horizon for his car. The road he had turned on ended at a clump of trees and a house.

"He must be in there," I said.

"He can't see us if we can't see him," Taka replied, slowing down and easing the Corolla off on the shoulder.

The mailbox was plain aluminum, battered like an old bucket. Name and address were spelled out in stenciled blue letters, none of the fancy press-on reflective kind:

ESTHER POMODORI

RR 3, BOX 187

PSYCHIC

SIX

❧

THE GOLDEN RING VAN-
ISHED, YET ANADEL'S CRY PULSED IN MY BONES. I LEFT
THE SLEDGE BUT KEPT THE PACK, AND STRUGGLED BACK
to the path, the axe in my hand. With the extra burden, my
return took twice as long as the journey out.

When at last I came out of the forest, I saw what I feared
before me: The door of the cottage was open. Were they dead,
then?

"Ana!" I cried. "Lily!" and I plunged into darkness. As my
sight cleared, I saw the table on its side, the bench broken, the
bed tick split and strewn.

"Nooooo!" a wail came out of me. "Nooooooo!"

A tiny voice answered. "Jamie?"

"Lily!"

"Here."

She was in the corner behind the grain sack.

"Are you all right, lass? Can you get up?"

She was not pinned beneath anything, but she shook her head, eyes shut tight.

"Where is Ana?"

"Bear," Lily said, her face in her hands.

"What did he do to her?"

No answer.

"Lily!" I put my hands on her shoulders. She kept her head down, and her yellow hair fell over her face. I wanted to shake her. Instead, I backed away and looked in every corner of the cottage to make certain Ana was not there. Then I came back and knelt before my sister.

"Lily," I said, taking her face in my hands. "Ana could be hurt somewhere. You have to tell me what happened."

Lily opened her eyes, but there was no light in them. "Bear," she said. "Bear took her."

~ 7 ~

✳

"*T*hat's enough," I said. "Let's get out of here!"

"She didn't *look* like a psychic," Taka observed, pulling back onto the road.

"What does a psychic look like?" I asked.

We were silent for a minute and then said, in the same oh-I-get-it voice at exactly the same time, "Like that."

We burst out laughing. We laughed and laughed, which hurt, because I *really* had to pee. Then, just like a switch had been flipped, I started crying. Taka thought they were laugh-tears at first. "You can stop now," she said. "It's not *that* funny."

I was sobbing. Big, ugly gasping sounds. It felt like my throat would break.

"Gina," Taka said, her voice gentle now. "This may be a good development."

We were getting back into traffic. A guy in a blue convert-ible passed us, honking his horn, and Taka almost ran off the road.

I kept crying.

"At least he's not having an affair," she said.

"How do you know?"

She didn't respond. She negotiated the turn into an old gas station that was now part mini-mart. When we were stopped at the pump, she reached over and patted my back. "I just don't think so," she said. "And neither do you. Take a deep breath," she commanded. "You're all right."

And I felt better. I dug for a Kleenex in my backpack, then blew my nose. "I'll go find the bathroom," I told her. "Meet you back here."

Someone had used enough Pine-Sol in there to choke a cat. It stung my nose. Still, on the way out, I stopped to splash cold water on my face and comb my hair. In the pocked and peeling mirror, I studied myself. Who was I? I sort of knew who I used to be, but who was I now? My mom had fled to North Carolina, my brother had divorced me, and now my dad, the sought-after surgeon, for God's sake, was out in a wheat field with a psychic. I stared into my own eyes. They looked so much like Mabry's. How could they see so differently?

Who you are is *Gina,* I told myself. Gina on her own. Who you are is sane. I straightened the collar of the blue shirt I was wearing over my purple tank top.

And I went out to the car to find that Taka had bought us a feast: coffee, orange juice, bananas, and those giant pastries called bear claws.

"Eat the banana first," she advised. "Otherwise all that sugar will make you feel weird."

"Mabry asked about you," I said as I bit into the pastry. Flakes of glaze fell on my lap like snow. "He can't believe a cool junior girl would hang out with his sister."

"I'm cool?" Taka asked, easing the Corolla back on the road.

SEVEN

I LAID THE BED TICK OVER
THE PALLET OF LEAVES, CARRIED LILY TO IT, THEN SET
ABOUT REKINDLING THE FIRE. BY HEAVEN'S MERCY, THERE
were embers under the ashes. These I fed with shavings whittled
from the wood I had brought. Soon I had blaze enough to lay
thin limbs on.

"It's fear-frozen you are," I said to Lily. "You will come back to
yourself once you get warm."

She smiled a half smile, but not at me. At the fire perhaps, or
her skin's delight in it.

I found a candle, lit it, and looked more closely at the room:
fireplace with the table and benches at one end, our food stores
and clothing at the other. Nothing was ruined. I could mend the
bench. Lily could stitch up the bed tick. And Ana—oh my God,
for a moment Ana's plight had left me! Warmth and hunger had
me bedazed. I must find food for us and be gone.

"Lily," I ventured, trying to keep fear from my voice. "There
was a loaf and cheese this morning. Do you know—?"

She pointed upward.

"No, Lily, the *food*. You must have something to eat."

Again she pointed toward the roof, and this time I followed her gesture.

A small sack was wedged in a fork of the rafters.

"'Tis there?" I asked.

She nodded.

"You climbed to get away from Bear?"

Again she nodded.

"Brave girl!" I said, and hugged her to me. Then, using the stones of the wall as steps, I climbed, grabbed a crossbeam, swung up, and reached to get the bundle. Looking down from Lily's perch, I began to shake, thinking of what she must have seen. I came down more slowly.

Once beside her, I opened the sack, took out the loaf, and broke us each a piece.

"Here, Lily." She did not reach to take the food, so I put it in her hand.

"Bear," she said.

"I know, lass. I know. But you got away from him. Did he hurt Ana?"

She shook her head. She sniffed the bread but did not eat it.

"What did the bear do?"

Lily reached over and stroked my hair, patted my face.

"Good," I said, though this made me shake again. "It did not hurt her."

Lily smiled.

"Was it a black bear?" I asked her.

She shook her head and looked away.

"Brown, then?" She looked at me, uncomprehending. "Like my boots, lass," I said, lifting my foot. "Like Da's jacket." I pointed to the coat I was wearing.

"Da!" Lily cried, hope lighting her face. She looked about the room frantically.

"No, no. He's not here. 'Tis still daylight. The bear, Lily. Was it brown?"

She hung her head like a hurt beast. Ana's face flashed before me.

"Lily!" She started from the force of my voice. I lifted her chin. "What did the bear look like?" Please God, I thought, let her tell me. And let it not be white.

For it had come to me, as I followed those tracks in my mind, that Da and the white bear might be one. It could not be, and yet he had said, "'Tis a witching world." Perhaps he left before light each day so none of us would know—

Lily's eyes focused for a second on mine. "Snow," she said. A cry rose in my throat but I held it back. She was so small, so frightened.

"There now," I said. "I'll split more wood for you and then I'll find Ana."

"And Da will be here with me?" Lily asked.

To hear her speak was great comfort, but her question! It tore at my heart! All I said was, "Lily, little one, I do not know."

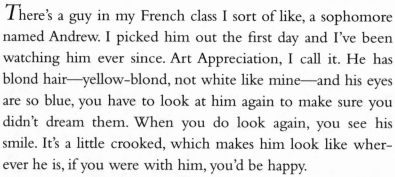

~ 8 ~

*T*here's a guy in my French class I sort of like, a sophomore named Andrew. I picked him out the first day and I've been watching him ever since. Art Appreciation, I call it. He has blond hair—yellow-blond, not white like mine—and his eyes are so blue, you have to look at him again to make sure you didn't dream them. When you do look again, you see his smile. It's a little crooked, which makes him look like wherever he is, if you were with him, you'd be happy.

At the beginning of school, when we were studying numbers, Mrs. Webb brought candy bars and French money and had us play store, *la confiserie.* She divided us into buyers, who got bills, and sellers, who got candy bars and coins. We were paired up and allowed to keep our books open to the store vocabulary, but we had to conduct the sale in front of the whole class. I was a seller, and Andrew was my customer.

"Bonjour," I said, thinking, I'm scared to talk to *you* in English.

"Bonjour," he answered. *"Je veux acheter du chocolat."*

He sounded pretty good and he looked adorable.

"Go on, Gina," Mrs. Webb prompted.

"Voulez-vous du Kit Kat *ou du* Hershey's?" I asked him.

"Kit Kat."

"S'il vous plaît," Mrs. Webb put in.

"S'il vous plaît," he repeated.

I started to hand it to him, but Mrs. Webb stopped me. "No, no. Andrew, ask her how much it is."

Andrew looked at his book. *"C'est combien?"* he asked, raising his eyebrows as if to say, I can't believe I'm doing this.

I looked at the label Mrs. Webb had stuck on the red wrapper. *"Aujourd'hui, c'est trois francs,"* I said.

He handed me a twenty-franc bill. That's when I noticed his hands. They're square. The thumb bone comes straight out from the wrist and makes a corner.

"Voici vingt francs," Andrew said, holding out the money.

I took the bill, then fumbled with the coins till I found the right change. Counting it into his hand, I thought, Money, you don't know how lucky you are.

I couldn't get *that* close to Andrew, but surely I could find a way to talk to him in our own language. Finding out Esther was a psychic gave me the break I'd been waiting for. I decided to work up my nerve and ask Andrew if he knew anything about them. This was not as bizarre as it sounds, because the week our vocabulary included the planets, he had asked Mrs. Webb what the word for "astrology" was.

"Qu'est-ce que c'est le mot pour 'astrology'?"

She laughed. "Probably *l'astrologie,*" she told him. "I don't know, Andrew. I don't know how to read palms, either."

Laughter. I thought she was being mean, but I looked at Andrew, and he didn't seem to mind. I was the one who was blushing. And writing in my mental notebook for Art Appreciation, "Interested in astrology."

So the day after Taka and I had read the words on that battered mailbox, I caught up with Andrew in the hall between classes and blurted out, "You like astrology?"

He smiled that smile, and my face got hot. I couldn't believe I was doing this.

"Not *like* it exactly," he said. "I just think there might be something to it. After all, if the moon can move the ocean—"

"What about psychics?" I butted in.

"Probably something there too," he said. "With some of them. Not the phone psychics," he went on. "They're a scam."

We'd gone down the stairway by that time and past the water fountain, and the door right ahead was my next class. Andrew was *talking* to me. He was walking down the hall and talking to me.

"What do *you* think?" he wanted to know.

"I think I've got to go in here," I said, and lunged for the door.

That night I was still thinking about Andrew when I took a break from homework and went downstairs to get a Coke. Dad was standing at the island in the kitchen making a cheese sandwich. "Gina!" he said, looking up from onion slicing. "How's my girl?"

Esther's red hair flashed across my mind. Who's your girl? I thought, but I just said, "Fine."

"Hungry?" He held out a slice of Swiss cheese.

"No thanks, Dad," I said, and he added the cheese to his sandwich. "I just came down for something to drink."

"That Lean Cuisine we had for supper didn't quite do it for me," he said.

"Mabry calls it doll food."

"He ate two Hearty Entrees," Dad pointed out, then took a paper plate and wicker holder from the stack on the island, cut his sandwich in half, and positioned it just so on the plate.

"He's a big doll," I said.

Dad is always arranging things. He never just puts something down. He places it. He wants us to do that, too. Once he got furious with Mabry because the drill was on the landing where the stairs turn. Mabe, who was maybe twelve at the time, was starting or finishing some project in his room and the drill was coming or going. Walking through the family room, I ran smack into this scene:

Dad, standing solemnly before the fireplace, hands on Mabry's shoulders. Dad, tall and imposing in his suit, though it was Saturday, his blue-black hair precisely combed. Mabry still a scrawny, towheaded kid.

"This is not how we do things, son," Dad was saying in a grave voice. "We take care of our tools. We finish things. You understand?"

Mabry nodded.

Dad held out the drill. "So use it or put it away," he said.

"But I was just between—" Mabry started.

"*Between* is the problem," Dad cut in. "Don't stop at *between*. Go all the way to *done*."

Mabry shrugged his bony shoulders. "I'll put it back," he said, resentment in his voice. Dad handed him the blue-plastic-cased drill as if it were the crown jewels. "See you," Mabry mumbled, heading for the garage.

"Wait!" Mom called from the kitchen. "Where are you going?"

"Baseball practice," Mabry yelled back, and was out the door.

The day this happened I thought it was just another example of Dad's weirdness. Mom said being a surgeon made him obsessed with order—you have to know exactly where *every-thing* is before you make a cut. But recalling the scene while Dad rinsed knives and put them in the dishwasher, while he scrubbed the cutting board and cleaned the counter before he even let himself *eat*, I saw something else: This wasn't just between Dad and us kids. This was a big issue for him and Mom, who was always "in process"—Dad's words—with everything. She'd be potting violets while cooking lasagna while making my North Star costume for the school play. So that scene with Mabry was being played out for Mom to see. He was trying to teach *her* a lesson, not just us! But he wanted to teach us too. He wanted to make sure we didn't turn out like her. . . .

Well, that sucks! It made me furious. I looked at Dad pouring Cascade into the little cup in the dishwasher door, and all my Noble Devoted Father feelings hit the wall. I wanted to rake his well-made sandwich and mug of beer off the counter. I wanted to grab the garbage can and dump it out at his feet. There'd be nothing loose and messy in it, though. At our house, everything organic that can't go into the disposal has to be zipped into a plastic bag before you throw it away.

Dad started the dishwasher and turned around, wiping his hands on a paper towel. He smiled. "A penny for your thoughts," he said.

What I thought was, This neatness freak is seeing a psychic? What would Andrew think?

What I said was, "I was thinking I need a bubble bath. It's been a long week."

EIGHT

T HE WIND HAD COME UP,
AND IT WAS SNOWING HARD AGAIN WHEN I WENT BACK
INTO THE WOODS. BUT THE ACHE OF COLD WAS NOTHING
compared with the pain of leaving Lily. So small she was, so
shaken. How would she fare alone? I had found but scant food in
the bundle. And, God in Heaven, what if Bear should come
back? What if he should take her, too? My mind battled these
thoughts the way my body battled the blizzard.

And my mind struggled with the blizzard as well. Perhaps it was
a dream, this world-whitening out of time? Perhaps I would wake
to blue skies and yellow leaves again, to birds feeding on berries that
redden the vine round our door. . . . I shook my head. No. Mine was
this frozen world, and I had to keep moving within it.

At first I could see the path I had been on before, the crevice
in the snow made by Da or Bear. I could keep to it well past the
treefall where I had worked. But light was waning even as snow
thickened, and soon all track of travel disappeared.

Still I plunged on. I could not go back. I had to find them. Bear.

Ana. Da. Even if Bear and Da were the same. No, I said. Such a thing cannot be! But there was, around that *No*, a knowing. It was Bear that Da did not want me to follow. These words, blazing in my head, kept me going. My eyes burned, my chest hurt, my cheeks felt like stone. But I stumbled farther and farther into the dark woods. I had promised Lily. . . . I had to save Ana. . . . I must face Da. . . . And then I stopped.

Or something stopped me. It was as if I were collared to a lead that I had stretched as far as it could go. When it jerked me back, I knew who I was. I knew what I was after. And I knew I was lost.

Panic was like a kicking child in my chest. I put my hand there. "Be still," I said. "I will take you home." Admitting failure, I turned to follow my own trail back. But there was no trail. Snow had healed that wound.

"Da?" I shouted, tears like a fist in my throat. "Da? It's Jamie!"

My voice made a path. Silence took it.

"Ana!" I screamed. "Where are you?"

My words swirled out, eaten by snow.

And then, on my knees, the glittering blanket up to my chin, I made one last ragged call. "Bear?"

And he was there.

Standing as a man stands, huge and gray-white. Ice edged his fur. He stepped from behind what I suddenly recognized as the Yew Tree and seemed to flow toward me, the snow no hindrance. I scrambled to my feet.

When he raised his shaggy arm as if to strike, breath left me. But there was no blow. Instead, he rested his great paw on my head, its weight like a roof beam. Neither of us made a sound. If we stand thus through the night, I thought, I will be sunk into the earth like a root.

But with his other paw, he tapped me on the shoulder and, all heaviness gone, I began spinning. Twirling like Anadel's spindle as it twists the thread. After a time, spinning gave way to dancing. Limbs free, I leapt like a flame in the midst of the frozen forest.

One tree Many branches In the hollow Bear dances

Warm at last, I forgot Bear, forgot all my quest, and was taken up by the Dance, used by it until, heat gone, it dropped me into the hollow heart of that tree.

~ 9 ~

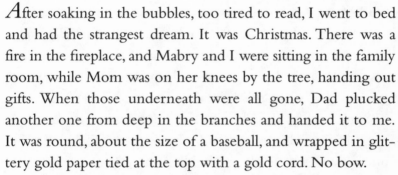

After soaking in the bubbles, too tired to read, I went to bed and had the strangest dream. It was Christmas. There was a fire in the fireplace, and Mabry and I were sitting in the family room, while Mom was on her knees by the tree, handing out gifts. When those underneath were all gone, Dad plucked another one from deep in the branches and handed it to me. It was round, about the size of a baseball, and wrapped in glittery gold paper tied at the top with a gold cord. No bow.

I shook the little gift and heard nothing, then opened it to find a snow globe. Small enough to fit in the palm of my hand, it held a forest scene. I could make out different kinds of trees and even a path through the deep snow. Wondering if the path would disappear, I shook the globe and heard a branch snap. I looked over to see what Dad could be doing to the tree.

But what I saw was snow.

Great clouds and windblown sheets of it, and through this,

our tree, rooted again and decorated only in white. Family and family room had vanished and I, in an oversize cloak, rough and smelling of wood smoke, stood on that path.

I woke up shivering at 3:00 A.M. I got out of bed and went to the window. No snow. It was October. *A dream,* I said to myself, shaking my head. You've had a dream! I went into the bathroom and splashed warm water on my face. (You're supposed to use cold, I know, but I was freezing.) Still, the dream coated me, the way bath oil sticks to your skin after you're out of the tub. I could smell pine trees, smoky cloth, cold. I remembered one tree in particular, taller than the rest, a ways ahead of me down the path.

Getting into bed, I still felt confused. What if I really *was* in the forest and only dreaming my room? What if I closed my eyes and thought I was going to sleep but was really waking up in that snowy world? I didn't want to!

I went back to the bathroom and drank some water. Mom always had me do that if I had a bad dream. "This will bring you around," she would say, holding the cup to my lips, patting my back, smoothing my long hair away from my face. And sometimes she would sing till I got back to sleep:

> *You'll never be the sun turning in the sky*
> *And you won't be the moon above us on a moonlit night*
> *And you won't be the stars in heaven*
> *Although they burn so bright*
> *But even on the deepest ocean*
> *You will be the light.*

Oh, Mom! Tears rose in my throat.

I turned on the radio to cover my blubbering, and then did something I hadn't done since she left. I reached up to the shelf where my dusty speech trophies were and got the stuffed bear she had bought me the last time we went to the zoo. He's yellow-white, like my hair, and I called him Orrie, for Ourisman. He was always on my bed until Mom left. Then I exiled him. But that night I felt he might keep me out of the snow globe. That night he was as close to Mom as I was going to get.

NINE

Still as a seed I lay in the hollow of the tree. Senseless. I do not know how long. Only there was light, the beginning of morning, coming from somewhere above as I woke up. After light, the first thing I knew was smell: heartwood, wet fur, and wild breath of Bear.

I sat up, the cushion of needles and leaves beneath me stirring. I got to my feet and looked all around. No Bear in this wide circle. Had I dreamed that dance?

If Bear was not here now, it was clear that he *had* been; I would go out and see what the snow told me. I looked for the door. No light gave it away. And then I remembered Da telling me of the Yew Tree with a room to which he had never found the door. Was this that tree? Had I come all the way to the center of the forest without knowing, without seeing the Ash Tree that marked its heart? My senses must have been swathed in snow. But whether this was Da's hollow tree or another, it had a way in, so there must be a way out. Carefully I walked the perimeter of the circle, using hands as well as eyes. Nothing. I felt the walls draw in, my breath speed up.

Stop, Jamie! I told myself. Think. I searched for my axe, hoping to chop a way out. I could not find it. Think, I insisted. How did you get in? But I had no memory. *Imagine*, then, I urged. And it came to me: Perhaps I fell. Perhaps where I stood was not level with the ground but beneath it, in a great taproot. Perhaps the light trickling in from above marked the door. And I began to climb. To pitiful effect at first. In my haste, I could not get a foothold and twice fell back. Then I forced myself to slow down, to look for the likeliest route, and I found it. Before long I was slipping out of a very narrow knothole in the tree.

White blinded me. I closed my eyes. A great growl shot them open again. Heart racing, I scanned the dazzling forest: no Bear. But I could hear—

Another growl and the force of a huge paw knocked me face-forward in the snow. Where had he come from? I scrambled to my feet but before I could focus my eyes, I was struck again. Claws tore my cheek. Every time I rose, Bear slammed me down, so I tried another motion. Kneeling, I bent into a ball and hurled myself forward. If I did not hit Bear, perhaps I would roll free. But I did. I struck his hind legs. And with all my furious strength, I bit into that white fur.

Bear roared.

And I roared back: "I want my sister! I want my Da!"

Bear did not strike me again. By way of answer, he leaned down and picked me up by the ankles. He held me facing away from him so that I was helpless to do him harm.

Clucking under his breath, he strode several yards through the snow to the Ash Tree. Vines wound around it, and these he pulled loose with his teeth. Brittle with cold, the vines should have broken, but they did not. And by any ordinary means, Bear should not have been able to turn me around, slip my feet beneath a loop of vine ten feet off the ground and, lashing more vines around them, bind me to the tree.

Blood rushing to my head addled me, and I made no struggle. I was staring at Bear's underbelly now, the white fur streaked and burr-snagged. He huffed as he labored. So easily he could kill me, but what he was doing was hard. Finished and turning away, he may have made a word of his breathing. The white Bear, He-Who-Does-Not-Sleep, who left me like a hide tied upside down to a tree, may have spoken, may have called my fading self "Son."

~ 10 ~

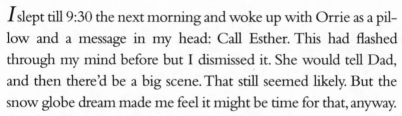

I slept till 9:30 the next morning and woke up with Orrie as a pillow and a message in my head: Call Esther. This had flashed
through my mind before but I dismissed it. She would tell Dad,
and then there'd be a big scene. That still seemed likely. But the
snow globe dream made me feel it might be time for that, anyway.

After pulling on jeans and a sweatshirt, I went downstairs
and found, much to my dismay, Dad in the breakfast room
reading the paper and eating an omelette.

"Morning, Glory," he said. That was strange. It was Mom's
mom, Grandma Pierce, who said that.

"Morning, Dad," I replied, thinking, *What* are you doing
here? The very morning I want to do something sneaky, you
stay home. "Sleep well?" I asked.

"Like a baby," he said, then chuckled. "Woke up every two
hours and cried."

"Dad!" This was going from strange to weird. Dad is not
the type of father who lounges around the house on Saturdays
cracking eggs and corny jokes.

As if reading my mind, he said, "Can I fix you an omelette? With onion and a sprinkling of dill?"

"No thanks, Dad," I said. I opened the cereal cabinet and got the granola.

I looked at him, sitting up straight at the breakfast table. His khaki pants were neatly pressed, his blue oxford-cloth shirt smooth, his black hair shiny as a grackle. His cuffs were rolled up, so I could see the springy hair at his wrists. I used to sit in his lap and try to clear the hair away from his big silver watch but, try as I would, it sprang back.

I asked him, as casually as I could, "So what are you up to today?" I put my bowl on the table, then got the milk and orange juice.

"Golf tournament," he said. "To benefit the Pain Clinic."

"But you don't *play* golf," I said, incredulous.

"Not very well," he admitted. "But that doesn't matter. The point is to collect the fees." He looked at his watch. "And I'd better get going," he said. "Tee time's ten-thirty."

"Good thing I didn't want that omelette," I joked.

He got up, rinsed all his dishes, including the omelette pan, and put them in the dishwasher. He wiped the counter. "What do you and Mabry have scheduled?"

"Mabe has a soccer game," I told him. "I just have homework. And practice. I might do that over at Taka's."

"Okay," Dad said. "Just put it on the chart."

That's another one of Dad's eccentricities. We can't leave messages on a bulletin board or on slips of paper on the counter. He's used to looking at charts in the hospital and says it makes sense to do it here, too. Efficient. So we have to write our whereabouts on drug-promo paper on a clipboard.

Dad finished cleaning up and rested his hand on my head. "See you at dinner," he said.

Weird gave way to bizarre: Dad touched me.

As soon as he was gone, I grabbed the phone and called information. "Akron" didn't work. "Atwater" didn't work. So I went to the map file in the study, unfolded Ohio, and looked for Route 377, the road Esther's house was on. Between the big city and the small town was another place in the tiniest print: TUXEDO, it said. Bingo.

"I have an Esther *Rose* Pomodori," the operator said.

Now that's helpful, I thought. Good to distinguish her from all those other Esther Pomodoris running around Tuxedo. "That's her," I said.

There were several clicks, and a computer voice declared, "The number is 403-555-7177."

So I called her. I did not get ready to call her. I did not have a cup of coffee, brush my teeth, jog up and down the stairs. I punched in the numbers as soon as I'd written them down.

"Hello," a woman answered.

"Is this Esther Pomodori?" I asked.

"Oh, yes," she said. "I'm so glad you called."

TEN

Winter upside down and Da below me. He is so tall, I must be a babe again. He rubs his eyes, turns and turns in the snowfall, growing smaller, shedding his fur coat. He stops. But 'tis so cold, Da. And are you leaving? A man, a mark, among the dark trees.

"No tears now," Ma says to me in her lap. "Da's gone hunting." She bounces me on her knee. "Upsy-daisy!" She leans us forward, my head at her feet. "So you were born," she says, and laughs, clapping my hands in her hands, strong, firelight flashing on her gold ring.

~ 11 ~

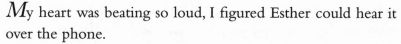

My heart was beating so loud, I figured Esther could hear it over the phone.

"Gina," she said, and the strangest thing: I felt like she could see me standing barefoot in the kitchen. Stranger still, I felt like I saw her in hers.

"Are your cabinets purple?" I asked.

She laughed. "Lavender," she said.

"Oh, God," I answered. Prayed, almost. What was going on here?

"Not to worry," she said. "We've just got a good connection."

"I think I need to see you."

"I think you already have," she said. Did she mean just now or that day we followed Dad to McDonald's?

"I mean . . . to *talk*," I said, fumbling for words. "I have questions."

"Of course," she answered, and her voice made me feel it was okay to have questions.

"When?" I asked.

"It's best not to miss more school," she said. At least I think she said *more*. Maybe I imagined it. "Could you come tomorrow?"

There had to be a way: Taka—or even Mabry—if I paid him. "Yes," I said. "What time?"

"One o'clock?" she suggested.

"Sure."

"You know how to find me?" Esther asked. Was there a smile in her voice?

I admitted I did. "You won't tell Dad?" I asked.

"You'll tell him," she said. "When the time comes."

"Is he okay?" I asked, my eyes suddenly stinging.

"Oh, Gina," she said, a rush of feeling in her voice. "Yes. And you are too."

ELEVEN

Though sun rises
day dims
as I hang
beholding great trees
grown upside down
into sky.
Furred by ice
peeled by the blade
of the wind
blood slow as tree blood
skin turning to bark.
"Think leaves," a voice
dreams to me.
"Think eggs, warm
and hidden
in a soft place."

~ 12 ~

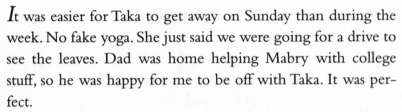

It was easier for Taka to get away on Sunday than during the week. No fake yoga. She just said we were going for a drive to see the leaves. Dad was home helping Mabry with college stuff, so he was happy for me to be off with Taka. It was perfect.

Still, I was so nervous before she showed up that I did something really strange. Strange for me, I mean. I called Andrew. He's Andrew Kephart Jr., so his number wasn't hard to find.

A woman answered—his mom, I guess.

"May I please speak to Andrew?" I asked.

"He's at church," she said.

Church? He goes to church? This surprised me. And if he went, why wasn't his mother there, too?

"I could have him call you when he gets home," the woman went on, filling in the silence.

"That would be great," I said. And then, "No, wait. I'm not going to be here. I'll just see him at school tomorrow."

"All right," she said, sounding skeptical. "Shall I tell him you called?"

"Please," I said. "And thanks."

As soon as the phone clicked, I realized I hadn't told her my name. I felt too dumb to call back, and anyway, Taka was at the door.

"Come on up to my room," I told her. "We've got a problem." I'd forgotten to ask Esther how much she charged, and I wanted to be sure I had some money. We pooled our cash and came up with forty-eight dollars. Then Taka said I might need a favorite object for Esther to hold.

"Why?"

"So she can get in touch with you," Taka said.

"Why would she need to get in touch with me? I'll be right there," I said.

"Gina," Taka said, "we need to get going. Just take my word for it, and grab something."

"Like what?" I asked.

"A piece of jewelry, a scarf," she said. "Something that means a lot."

"But I'm allergic to jewelry. You know that. It makes me break out."

"What about your ring?"

"I wear it because I can't get it off," I reminded her.

"Oh, yeah," Taka said. "Good thing it's your bowing hand. So bring a scarf," she advised, looking over the junk on my dresser top.

"Taka, when did you ever see me wear a scarf?"

"Never," she admitted, then pointed to the music stand in the corner.

"What about the cloth you polish your viola with?"

"A rag?! I can't give her a rag!"

"Well, *you* think," Taka said, sitting on the bed. "You've got to give her something." Then she saw Orrie, who was still on my pillow. "What about this?" she asked.

"Mom gave it to me," I told her.

"Perfect," Taka said, handing me the bear. "Let's sublime." We laughed. She'd been using the word all week. Her physics teacher told them it's what ice cubes do in the freezer when they disappear.

We sped down the highway, Taka singing, "We're off to see the Psychic, the wonderful Psychic of Tuxedo."

"That doesn't fit," I said, but I couldn't help laughing.

"No wonder," she said. "Tuxedos are for men."

"Does that mean only Dad should go there?"

"Are you getting scared?" she asked.

"No," I said firmly.

"Good."

"I'm already scared."

We arrived at Esther's mailbox at 12:45, having made a pit stop in Akron. Taka turned carefully onto the gravel road. When we passed it the first time I hadn't noticed it was lined with boulders. "That took a lot of work," I said, trying to keep my teeth from chattering.

"Unless they fell from the sky," Taka said.

I didn't smile.

"I don't think so," she said. "It would have made the papers."

Esther's house was small and white, with a front porch and a swing. In front of the rail a few late sunflowers stood, their leaves brown, their seeds picked over by birds. As we walked up, Esther came out the screen door. She was wearing jeans and a layered shirt, snowflake lace over yellow. Her hair was tied back, and her face had lots of fine lines.

"Welcome," she said, holding the screen door open. She looked at Taka. "And you are—?"

"Sorry," I said. "This is my friend, Taka Yamamoto. She can drive." I couldn't believe how dumb I sounded.

"So I see," Esther said. "Come on back to the kitchen."

We followed her through a small living room and dining room, both neat and—I don't know—*regular,* and then we came to the kitchen. Lavender cabinets, plum-colored walls, a wooden table shiny with rose paint. The back door was yellow. There was a clay pot full of orange berry-flowers on the table.

"Bittersweet," Esther said, following my gaze. I stood there feeling ridiculous, holding a stuffed bear.

"Are you going to do this together?" Esther asked. The teakettle whistled, and she reached over to turn off the stove.

"Not together," Taka said. "But can I stay?" She looked at me.

"It would probably work better if you didn't," Esther said.

"Then I'll just walk around outside," Taka told her.

I wanted to say, Don't leave me, but didn't. I'd trusted Esther this far. It was the only way I knew to reach Dad.

"Back in an hour?" Taka asked.

"That's good," Esther told her, and Taka slipped out the yellow door.

Esther poured boiling water into a blue teapot.

"Go on and have a seat, Gina," she said. "Or if you need a bathroom first, it's just down the hall." She gestured to a third door leading from the kitchen.

"No thanks. I'm fine."

Suddenly I started shaking. What had I gotten myself into?

"Did someone at McDonald's tell you we'd been looking for you?" I blurted.

"Robyn did, yes," Esther said, uninterested. She put the pot and two mugs at the end of the table. "This is orange tea," she said. "No caffeine." She sat down opposite me. "Let me see your hands," she said.

I held them out, palms up, expecting her to read them like maps. Instead, she reached over and took them in hers. I was embarrassed at first, but her hands were warm, and it felt *so* good. Her eyes were closed. I closed mine too. No sound but the refrigerator's hum. Then I felt a pulse in my hands. Was it hers or mine? I could feel my hands getting hot. From her? From me?

I don't know how long we sat like that. Time sort of disappeared, and I felt like I was floating, till Esther said, "Good," and very slowly let go of my hands.

I opened my eyes. I felt great. "Now can we talk about Dad?" I asked.

"Soon," she promised. "Let me get a better sense of you first."

I nodded.

"Are you comfortable?"

As comfortable as I can be in a psychic's kitchen, I thought. "Yes," I said.

She poured tea for us in yellow mugs.

"Now say your full name," she told me.

"Gina—"

"Isn't that a nickname?"

"Regina Hannah Ourisman," I told her, aware of my voice tightening up. I hate my whole name. It sounds like a boat company.

Now Esther's eyes were closed. Without their green-gold light, her face was a mask. "It's a beautiful name," she said, eyes still shut. "A complex energy."

Here we go, I thought.

"Imagination," she said, touching her forehead. "And *anger,"* she said, striking her diaphragm with her fist. "And *this,"* she said, eyes open now, her hand, fingers splayed, on her chest. "This torn heart."

I couldn't say anything for a minute. This wasn't fair. I put my hands in my lap, holding on to Orrie. Finally I blurted, "But I came about Dad!"

She smiled. Gently. I don't know how to say this, but it wasn't her smile. It wasn't just her smile. There was more.

"You're looking for something," she said.

"For my dad. I told you."

"And he's been looking for something too," Esther said. "But he's not been able to find it. I have a feeling, Gina, that you're supposed to help him. Would you do that?"

"I just want Dad back—"

"That's what it's about," Esther broke in. "Your dad and a part of you, too."

"I don't see what *I* can do."

"Just trust me," Esther said. "Go through a relaxation exercise and see what happens."

"Okay," I said. Just play along, I said to myself. Trade this for talking about Dad.

"Do you have something I could hold?" she asked.

I gave her Orrie.

Esther shut her eyes again. Mine shut too. She had me take several deep breaths, focusing on different parts of my body and letting the tension go. She started with my toes and worked her way up to the top of my head. "Do you feel relaxed?" she asked.

"Mm-hmm," I said. I felt light and sleepy.

"Good. Now picture yourself walking on a country road."

Without willing it, I leaned back in the chair and the warmth in the room drained away. All at once I was really cold, as if an icy wind were blowing. "Could it be in the woods?" I heard myself asking.

"Wherever you see it," she said.

I saw the snow globe world. I didn't want to be there.

"Look at your feet," Esther said, and I knew not to open my eyes. "What are you wearing?"

"Boots," I said. "I'm so cold."

"It's all right," she said, her voice soothing. "It's all right to be cold. Can you tell what clothes you're wearing?"

"A cloak," I said, my voice getting higher. "Brown wool. Over a tunic. The cloak has a hood—rough against my cheek. I'm on this path."

"Yes," she said, her voice farther away.

"I'm walking—deep snow—deep woods—Esther!" Suddenly I was crying.

"Go on, Gina. Go on."

"I can't see the path!"

"Don't look for it, then. Look around."

"There's one tree ahead—"

"Yes?"

"Something's *on* it. The light is not good. I can't tell—"

"Go closer," Esther urged. "Keep looking."

"There's something on the tree," I said again. My throat hurt.

"What is it?"

"It's like a cocoon."

"From an insect?" Was I asking this? Was Esther?

"It shouldn't be there!" I said vehemently.

"No."

"It's tied! Someone's tied it to the tree!"

"Do you have a knife?"

"I don't know. I'm not—"

"Check your belt, your pockets."

"Yes!" My heart was racing. I forgot the cold.

"So what can you do?"

"Cut it down?" I was close to the tree now.

"That would be good," the voice said.

"I can't reach it. I can't! It's above me." Breathing was hard now. I was striking at the bark with my knife.

"What can you do?" Esther asked again.

"Climb," I answered. And, stabbing the knife into the tree as far above me as I could, I began to pull myself up. Wresting the knife free, I pierced the tree again, high above me, and kept climbing. Lungs aching, I finally reached the top of what had been tied to the tree. I knew what it was.

"Cut it loose!" Esther said.

I hacked at frozen vines with the knife in my hand. I tore with my teeth. I sawed and peeled and yanked till I pulled it free.

And fell far back into black with my treasure in my arms.

TWELVE

Voice like a faraway bird. "It's a boy!" Hands and breath on my face.

She rubbed my fingers and toes. She wrapped her whole self around me. Heat began to fade, but she was fierce. Fought. And brought it back. To her. To me.

I opened my eyes to see the pale face above me. Ma? Ana? An angel? None of these.

"Shelter!" she said. "We've got to get out of this wind!"

I tried to answer. My mouth slid over the shape.

She put her lips on mine.

"Rockhouse," I said, when she sat up. I pointed to the hill behind her.

She stood and tried to pull me to my feet. We both fell. She struggled up, tried again and again, till I was standing. Unable to feel the ground, I staggered.

"Lean on me," she said, and put my arm over her shoulder.

We started up the path.

~ 1 3 ~

❁

Stone eyelid, I thought when I saw it. Bizarre, but that's really what the rockhouse looked like. Not deep as a cave, but deep enough to be dry and keep the wind off.

I helped the boy sit. He was shaky and sweating, which scared me. What could I do?

As my eyes learned the dark, I looked around. Leaves had blown in and were piled toward the back. I stooped, then crawled, gathering them in my arms. The boy needed a place to lie down. I heaped the leaves beside him. "A bed for you," I said.

He smiled and shivered. His ink-black hair was scraggly, his eyes gray-blue. Wind and my hands had rubbed his cheeks red.

"What's your name?" I asked him.

But he just lay down in the nest.

Going back for more leaves, I found a little woodpile. And the wood was dry! I couldn't believe it. Okay. You rub sticks together and get sparks and catch twigs on fire. . . . We had done this at camp. Or watched somebody do it.

When I carried the wood and leaves to the front of the

rockhouse, I found a dug-out place with ashes in it. Yes! I heaped some leaves and twigs there, then arranged the wood so air could get around it. I rubbed and rubbed and rubbed sticks together, but the only thing that burned was my wrists. The rest of me was freezing, and my fingers would hardly bend. Think! I said to myself. How else do you get fire?

Sticks and stones. Something to do with stones. The boy would know. I crawled over to where he was sleeping, curled on his side, arms crossed on his chest. The cloth of his coat was tufted and knotted. Someone had made it, I thought. My God! Not just the coat but the cloth! I looked at my cloak. It was like that too.

I put my hand on his thin shoulder and shook him.

"Bear!" he said, sitting up so fast, he knocked me backward.

"Not a bear," I said, righting myself, my heart pounding. "I'm a girl."

And he laughed! This frozen, bedraggled boy. And I laughed too.

"I'm trying to start a fire," I told him. "Sticks aren't working."

He opened his coat and took two stones from the drawstring pouch at his waist. "Flint," he said.

I held out my hand. "Go back to sleep now," I said, and he did.

Clumsily, I struck the rocks together close to the leaves. Nothing. I tried again. Just a dull clink. A hundred more times, I told myself. Count backward. Ninety-nine . . . sixty-eight . . . forty-three . . . my shoulder blades ached . . . thirty-seven . . . sparks!

At first there was just a crackling, then fire flickered in the leaves. Twigs caught, followed by the smallest branches. A miracle!

Warmth stung my legs and arms. Then it made me giddy. I crawled over to the boy. "We won't die here!" I told him.

Spreading my cloak over us both, I curled up close. Heat held us. Rockhouse rocked us. As I slipped into sleep, I heard my mother's song:

> *You may not always shine*
> *As you go barefoot over stone.*
> *You might be so long together*
> *Or you might walk alone.*
> *And you won't find that love comes easy*
> *But that love is always right.*
> *So even when the dark clouds gather*
> *You will be the light.*

I woke up stretched out on the couch in Esther's kitchen. She must have led me there and let me rest. Taka had come back and was drinking tea at the table. Esther was cooking. I started to sit up.

"Just lie there a minute," she said. "You need to come back slowly."

I looked for Orrie. He was tucked in the crook of my arm.

"You okay, Gina?" Taka asked, turning toward me.

"What happened?" I asked Esther.

"You don't remember?"

I shut my eyes. The woods—the snow—

"No!" I said, so loud that Taka spilled her tea. "I mean, yes, yes. But what was it?"

"A soul journey," Esther said, wiping the table at Taka's elbow. "It's important that you remember."

I sat up slowly, realizing Esther had covered me with a quilt. "Did you go with me?" I asked her. I felt dizzy. The bright room hurt my eyes.

"No," she said, dropping cut-up carrots into a soup pot. "But I was in touch with you. It's like when a diver goes off a ship but has an air line. I wasn't *with* you, but I was connected and knew where you were."

"You couldn't see. . . ."

"No," she said, stirring.

"The thing on the tree—the husk I had to cut down?" I heard the urgency in my voice.

"What are you talking about?" Taka asked, concern giving an edge to her voice.

"It was a task," Esther explained. "A rescue Gina had to perform. And she did it. You remember that, Gina?"

"Yes," I said. "But why? Where was I?"

"In your subconscious?" Taka asked, intense. "Or your unconscious?"

Esther rinsed celery at the sink. "Or in another dimension," she said. "Another lifetime. Another level of this life."

"But is it real?" Taka asked. She was braiding her hair, a sure sign she was worried.

Esther turned the question to me. "Was it real, Gina?"

"Yes, but—"

"Just focus on the *yes*," she said, chopping again.

"But it was a *boy*, Esther. A boy I cut down."

"That's good," she said. "That's what you went for."

"But why? And where is he now?" I asked.

"Have you ever been to Toledo?"

"Sure," I said.

"But you're not there now."

"No."

"So where is it?" Esther asked.

I didn't answer. My head hurt.

"It's right where she left it," Taka said. "Cities don't go anywhere."

"How do you know?" Esther asked.

"This is stupid!" I said. I got up and came to the table.

Esther wiped her hands, brought me a glass of water, and sat down, too. "You really think so?" she asked. She reached over and gave the bittersweet a little turn.

"No," I said, and sipped some water. Then I knew I was thirsty. I drank it all.

"Good girl," Esther said. Taka got up and refilled my glass.

"But what has that boy got to do with Dad?"

"I'm not certain," Esther admitted. "He'll have to tell us."

That made me mad. "What are you *doing?*" I asked, leaning toward her, my hands on the table. "How did you meet Dad, anyway? Why does he come here?"

Esther, cool and calm, said, "It goes back a ways. About five years ago I met your mother at a Whole Health Fair. I traded her a reading for a yoga tape. Then I did Dream Work with some of her students at the studio. When things started falling apart at home, she tried to get your dad to see me—"

"But he had more sense than that! I remember him saying, 'Dreams are just your mind taking out the trash.'"

Taka put her hand on my wrist. "Gina—"

"It's all right," Esther said. "She needs to get it out."

"Ooooooo!" I said, furious suddenly. "That's so condescending!"

"Gina—" Taka's voice was insistent.

"What?" I snapped at her.

"Your ring. The one you can't get off. It's gone."

THIRTEEN

❧

It was late morning when I awoke in the rockhouse. But what morning? Bone-sore, I sat up. How long since I left Lily to look for Bear? Two nights? Three? The food would have lasted but a day, and Lily, weak and asleep, might have let the fire go out. And I had not returned to her. I had found Bear, but that was useless, for I had not found Ana. I was no rescuer. I had failed them.

Then I remembered: It was I who had been rescued. The girl had cut me down from the tree, warmed me, and given me speech with her breath. She had brought me to the rockhouse. Where was she? I wanted to find and thank her. But she was gone. Nothing remained of her work, nothing but ashes. And me, called Jamie.

My body and clothes were dry, and Da's jacket lay stretched on a stone by the fire-pit. My boots were there, too, and I hastened into them. Heavyhearted though I was, recalling the girl gave me hope. Something buzzed in my ears. Like a bee in clover in that winter-held world. It filled my head and left no room for weeping. "Home," it hummed.

The journey back was not so arduous. I knew where I was. It was morning, and I had had my fill of sleep. Food, too, in some fashion, for I was not hungry. The path seemed wider, and I sped along it.

But as I neared the cottage, fear again squeezed my heart. What would I find there? If Lily was alive, how could I confess my failure? And if she was not—God in heaven, what then?

Still, the drone sounded in my ears and, like a bear to honey, I hove home.

~ 1 4 ~

❀

Taka was worried as we hit I-77. We had been gone a lot longer than she'd said we'd be.

"Call your parents and let them know when you'll be there," I suggested. After what I'd been through, it didn't seem like a big deal.

"Not possible," she said.

"Why not?"

"My dad's at some kind of faculty retreat till seven," she said.

"So? Talk to your mom."

"Gina—" Taka sounded exasperated. Her foot was getting heavier, too. The reading on the speedometer matched the interstate number. "My mom doesn't have the vocabulary."

"You don't have to tell her about Esther—"

"Not *that* kind of vocabulary!" she said, as though I were a dunce. "English!"

"Don't bite my head off," I said. "How was I supposed to know?" I could feel myself all wound up from what had happened at Esther's. I didn't want to fight with Taka, but hurtful words were right there on my tongue. "I don't know *your* mom like you knew mine!"

"You didn't know your own mom very well, either," she shot back.

"Taka!" I saw all my mother's suitcases, her project bags, and yoga mat set beside the kitchen door. And my side hurt, as if the door was there.

Taka flipped her hair over her shoulders. She looked defiant. "Your mother wanted you, and you didn't even *try* to go with her."

"That's what you think." I heard the anger in my voice, but I didn't care. "And how could I leave Dad and my friends and go to North Carolina with some strange man?"

"It wouldn't have been with some strange man," Taka insisted. "It would have been with Meg. Your mother."

"She said I should stay here and go to Shaker Heights. It's such a good school—"

"So this is about education," Taka said, taunting.

"Mom didn't want me!" I said bitterly. "If she had, she would have gotten custody!"

"She *couldn't,* Gina," Taka said. "The lawyer told her it was hopeless, with your dad a doctor and her already involved with somebody else."

"How do you know that?"

"Because I came early to class one day, and she was sobbing. I asked what was wrong, and she was so upset that she told me. She'd just gotten off the phone."

But so what? So what if she had thrown away her legal

rights, too? "Either way, it was her choice!" I said fiercely. "However it worked out, she chose Whit over us."

"You're like my mom," Taka said, her hands tight on the wheel. "You just don't have the vocabulary for this kind of talk."

"And *you're* the expert," I said, but it didn't faze her.

"At least Mom has the words in Japanese," she went on.

"Taka, what are you talking about?"

"I could talk to her when we first moved here," she said, "but now my Japanese is fading. And Mom's English quit growing a long time ago. So we misunderstand each other a lot, especially on the phone. That's why I can't call her."

"That's wild," I said.

Taka didn't answer. She ran the back of her hand over her cheek like maybe there was a tear there.

I waited.

She drove.

We were getting back into Cleveland now, I-77 flowing into 480, lanes and cars multiplying. Taka was still driving fast, darting among SUVs and semis like a fish.

Finally I said, "But that's *your* mom. What's vocabulary got to do with mine?"

I expected this to float in silence a while, but Taka answered fast. "You say she chose Whit over you. What about life over death?"

"She wasn't *dying!*" I said, furious. "She had *everything*—"

"That's your dad talking," Taka told me.

Whoa! I felt like she'd hit me in the stomach.

"You know how I met your mom?" Taka went on.

"At her yoga class," I said. "I was there, remember?"

"And I was taking yoga because my dance teacher said my spirit wasn't in my body. When I told Meg, she said, 'I know that problem all right!'"

"How?" I asked. "Mom wasn't split like that."

Taka didn't miss a beat. "What about your dad?"

I didn't answer.

"Meg said the problem was serious because the longer body and spirit were separated, the more energy you lost and the harder it was to find your path."

"That's Mom. The Energy Queen."

"Is that you talking, Gina? Or is that your dad again."

Now I *couldn't* answer. This was too much. I felt her questions pressing into my throat. What had happened at Esther's? What was I searching for? I'd gone to find Dad, but there was that thing bound to the tree, that boy—

"Speaking of your dad," Taka said, breaking through the haze, "you're home."

There we were in the driveway, and I didn't even remember getting off the interstate.

"Thanks, Taka," I said, aware now that tears were running down my cheeks. "I mean, big-time thanks. And good luck when you get home."

"Hai!" she said. "I'll need it."

Then, just as I was about to close the car door, she said, "Will you tell your brother about this?"

"Mabry? He already thinks I'm crazy."

"Yeah, but I'm older. Tell him I said it was real."

FOURTEEN

THE FIST OF MY HEART
OPENED WHEN I SAW SMOKE RISING FROM THE CHIMNEY.
I CAME IN THE DOOR REJOICING. DA WAS THERE, THERE
seated at the table! And Anadel by him! And Lily stirring the
fire! I ran and threw my arms about his neck. "You are here, Da!
Praise the angels, you are home!"

He did not move.

I pulled back. I looked at his face, memorized before I had
speech. "Da? It's Jamie!"

The face was like stone.

And then, God help me, I struck him in the chest. "You speak
to me!" Another blow. "You say my name!"

A net of sister-arms came over me, pulling me back.

"Leave off, Jamie!" Ana cried. "He cannot help it."

"Aye. He's lost," Lily said, her voice soft as a dove's.

I wheeled around, pushing them from me. "NO!" I roared.
"He is not lost!"

My fierceness frightened Lily, and she began to cry. I put my arms about her. "There now," I said. "It is daylight, Lily, and he has not disappeared into the woods. He is here, our own Da. How can he be lost?"

~ 15 ~

❊

Dad must have been watching for me. He had the door open before I'd dug out my key. "*There* you are!" he said. Then, putting his arm around my shoulder, he drew me in. "Hungry?" he asked as he closed the door.

I nodded. Was he really not mad? We walked into the kitchen, where the table was set and soup was on the stove. It was potato soup, rich and creamy.

"So how were the leaves?" Dad asked.

"Leaves?" I was getting the milk out of the refrigerator, glad he couldn't see my face.

"You and Taka went driving to look at the leaves," he prompted.

"Oh yeah," I said, with a shaky laugh. "They were pretty, you know. Red and gold."

With a stainless steel ladle he filled our bowls, then brought them to the table. Bread was in its basket, salad in the wooden bowl.

"Where's Mabry?" I asked.

"Out on a date," he replied. "At some warehouse place called Climb Time. Just imagine if I had asked your mother to go wall climbing!" He looked rueful. Usually if he mentions Mom, he's mad.

I took a spoonful of soup. Too hot, it burned my tongue. Can't eat, might as well talk, I said to myself. I took a deep breath. "Dad," I began, "you're worrying me."

"Me?" He looked shocked.

"You leave here very early lots of mornings and you don't go to work."

He was buttering the last of his bread slice. He put down the knife. "Where I go and what I do is my business, Gina, as long as I provide for and take care of my children. And I'm doing that, aren't I?"

He gestured with his hands, palms up, at the table, as if homemade soup said it all.

"Mom took care of us, too, when she was sneaking around with Whit."

I hadn't meant to say that. I'd never let on like I knew.

"I can assure you," Dad said, cold as a surgical knife, "I am *not* behaving like your mother."

He never says her name.

"Besides, I couldn't have an affair if I wanted to." He gave a fake laugh. "I'm not married!"

I made myself take a bite of bread and chew it slowly. I drank some milk. Then I changed tactics. "Dad, if something really big was going on in my life—or Mabe's—wouldn't you want to know?"

"Of course. You're my children."

"You're my father," I said. "I want to know too."

I felt the plea in my voice. He ignored it.

"Parent to child is different from child to parent," he explained, in that you-are-slow-but-you-can-get-this voice he reserves for me. He stirred his soup. It was still too hot to eat. "Parents need privacy, and children shouldn't be burdened with adult affairs." He heard himself. *"Concerns,"* he corrected.

To avoid looking at him, I reached for the wooden spoons and helped myself to salad. "I'm not a child," I said. "And whatever you do is going to burden me plenty. Witness the divorce."

"*That* was your mother's doing!"

"Dad," I said. "I spent the afternoon with Esther."

Dad got up and left the table. Without a word, he went out the side door into the cold and dark. I didn't follow him. I'd done that already, and look how mad he was.

Mom had slammed out that door a few times. It had always scared me. Would she just go to the studio? Would she come back? Dad had never done it before. And he didn't slam it this time, either. Just closed it securely. He was the rational, level-headed one. Like Mabry, I thought. And Taka. Did I go *looking* for these people?

I tasted the soup. Dad was getting to be a good cook, and I was hungry, but I couldn't eat.

A whole other version of my story was tugging at me. Not the one about the father who was acting weird, but the one about the daughter. The *daughter* who was acting weird because she was so scared they'd all go out that door. Mom had . . . Mabry would . . .

I heard the front door key turn. Dad had just gone around the house. He didn't come straight back to the kitchen, though. First he went into his study, got something out of a drawer, then appeared with a brown envelope. He smelled cold, clear.

"I'm sorry," I said.

Dad sat down. He moved his plate and soup bowl and put the envelope in their place. "You followed me?" he asked. "You and Taka?"

I nodded.

"You were out driving the interstate and the back roads when I thought you were here or in school?"

"Just a few times." Here it comes, I thought. Bits of arguments between him and Mom, fights they had had at this same table came back to me. I could hear Dad's icy voice. "You *said* you would call. . . ."; "You never told me you were going to . . ."; "If you would just *think,* Meg, before you do these things. . . ."

"I guess you were desperate," Dad said. He laid his hands flat on the envelope. He took a measured breath. "I was, too," he confessed, handing me the envelope. "This is why."

I took it and undid the clasp. Nothing in there but a newspaper clipping. I fished it out and read:

AKRON TEEN DIES IN WRECK

There was a picture of a skinny blond kid, kind of punk-looking. Some patient Dad couldn't save? The article said:

Christopher James "Kit" McFerran, 19,
son of Jewel McFerran, Forest Cove, died
Friday of injuries received when he lost
control of his 1983 Ford pickup and hit a
tree on Elk Run Road.

I looked at the date. It was four years earlier. Was somebody suing Dad for malpractice? "Who is this?" I asked.

Dad didn't say anything. I laid the article in front of him and put my hand on his arm. "Dad?"

He shook his head. He touched his throat. Finally he took a pen from his shirt pocket and wrote on the clipping, in blue ink, above the date: Your Brother. My Son.

FIFTEEN

ANADEL, KNEADING BREAD, SAID THAT BEAR HAD NOT HARMED HER, ONLY FRIGHT-ENED HER INTO A STUPOR SO THAT SHE DID NOT REMEMBER being carried through the frozen woods. "I did not return to myself," she said, "until Bear, who had been clutching me to his chest, went down on all fours to enter a cave. Then I held on tight, clinging to the fur of his underbelly, as he padded through narrow dark until we came to a room. I could feel its roundness and the presence of another bear."

"What happened then?" I asked.

She scooped more flour onto the board and gave the dough a turn. "Bear rolled on his back," she said, "as easily as a dog might, and with his front paws, lifted me free of him. Then, gently as if I were a babe, he set me close by the other bear."

"What did you do?"

"I entreated him not to go," she said, "for suddenly he was not my captor, but my guide, the only way back. He nosed me, mak-ing clucking sounds deep in his throat. For a moment I thought he would take me up again, but then he turned and ambled off."

"Did you try to go after him?" Lily asked, breathless, though she must have heard all this before.

"No," Ana said, greasing a bowl before settling the dough ball to rise. "The heat of the sleeping bear, and its comforting smell, drew me into sleep as well, and I knew nothing more until Da appeared."

"Da?" I asked, astonished.

"Oh, yes," she said. "It was Da who fetched me home. He carried a small torch, and a piece of rope that he tied about his ankle for me to hold as I crawled out behind him. As now, he could not talk, and he wanted me to stay close, lest I turn down the wrong tunnel and be lost."

"If Bear cannot have Ana, maybe he wants something else," Lily said matter-of-factly. She spread my hand out in her lap and stroked it like a cat.

"Jamie!" Ana exclaimed. "That ring!"

A gold band circled my little finger. Though it looked tight, it slipped from my finger easily. I looked inside. *One tree* There was the woman in the vision *Many branches* and the girl who saved me. Could this ring open like the one I looked through in the rockhouse? Could it give Da speech? The girl had freed my voice with her breath. Please God, I thought. May it please God—

I got up from my stool by the fire and went over to Da. I knelt beside him, putting my hand on his knee.

Then I took the ring and, moving by memory, lifted it and kissed it. I felt a shimmer, like sound, like heat, on my lips. Holding the golden O before my eye, I looked at Da, and spoke:

"One tree
Many branches.
In the hollow
Bear dances."

And I could see *into* the ring. I saw the girl who had saved me at table with her father in a room white as snow. I saw her touch his cheek. Da turned his head.

And words came to me. I called on Bear:

"Angry One
Apple of the Forest
Big Great Food
Dweller in the Wilds

                      Listen!

Food of the Fire
Four-Legged Man
Golden Friend
Good-Tempered Beast

                      Give Back!

Honey Paw
Illustrious Pride
Owner of Earth
Sacred Man

                      His Tongue!"

Da's hand went to his mouth. His lips moved. There was a rasp. "Jamie."

~ 16 ~

⁂

"*I*'m sorry," I said, and touched Dad's cheek. He still didn't speak, so I went on. "This boy—Kit—was before you met Mom?"

He nodded.

"And you knew him?" I'd read about men having two families, two lives.

Dad shook his head. He cleared his throat. "I was a first-year med student," he began. "Jewel worked in the hospital cafeteria. We would talk over bad coffee late at night. She was a *good* person: sweet, generous, and funny. I used to tell her that I was taking anatomy to find out how they got such a big heart in such a small body."

Please, I thought. That's not the part I want to know.

"She was a lot like your mother in some ways. She loved to cook and garden, she loved hiking, but she wasn't interested in books. Her dream was a house in the country and lots of kids—" Dad's voice broke.

"But she only had Kit?" I asked.

He nodded. "I heard there were complications at the birth," he said. "I don't really know. I wasn't"—pain flashed across his face—"this is what I'm so ashamed of, Gina. He was my child, like you and Mabry, but when I found out Jewel was pregnant, I just wanted out. I gave her money. I got the name of a doctor who did abortions. 'I thought you were learning to *save* lives!' she said. 'I guess *I* have to save this one.' That was when we parted ways.

"After Kit was born, I set up a trust fund. I hardly had any money, but there was always some there for them. There always has been."

It was my turn at silence.

"But I never even saw Kit till Jewel sent the clipping in the mail."

Dad looked sick and exhausted. I didn't know what to say. How would you feel if your father didn't even want to *see* you?

Dad held up the envelope. "No return address, no note, but it had to be from Jewel. No one else knew the connection."

"Not even Mom?"

"Especially not your mom. It was a huge shock to her."

"I guess so." It's a pretty big shock to *me,* I thought. And *Mabry . . .*

"See, I'd walled all that off," Dad said, getting to his feet, "which is what you can't do." He picked up our bowls. "I'm going to reheat the soup, Gina. We need to eat." He turned the burner on under the soup pot and poured our share back in. "I told myself it was 'just one of those things,'" Dad said. "I had gotten sidetracked, somehow, and this unfortunate thing had happened. I never considered marrying Jewel. She wasn't 'suitable' for a doctor's wife, that's what I thought. I had this image of my life, you see."

And was I part of that image? I wanted to ask. But we were silent till the soup began to bubble.

"And then I met your mother, and fell in love, and never looked back," Dad went on, ladling out soup again. "If I had, I would have seen Kit. And what I had done to Jewel. If I had made things better somehow, maybe Kit would still be here." He brought the bowls back to the table.

"Lots of kids get killed in car wrecks," I told him. "Remember Ray Harbour?" Ray had been in Mabry's class since preschool. "He and his dad did all kinds of things together. They went hunting. They played golf. They even worked on the car Ray got killed in."

All Dad said was, "Mr. Harbour is lucky to have those memories."

We were quiet for a while, eating our soup. I felt sort of light-headed.

Then Dad said, "Jewel wouldn't see or talk to me after Kit died. I can't blame her. I needed to talk to somebody, and your mother listened for a while, but it was hard. She said I should put my attention *here, now*—and she was right. But I couldn't."

"Why didn't you try a therapist?" I asked.

"I did," Dad said, "for six months. And that helped me see some things. But it didn't touch the pain. Your mother gave me Esther's number and said I should see her. 'Sometimes your *spirit* needs a doctor,' she told me. I refused, of course. Even ridiculed the idea. But then Meg was gone, too. And after about a year, I called Esther. I thought if there *was* a Beyond, and I could find Kit and ask his forgiveness—well, then, maybe I could live with myself and go on."

I was just about to ask, Did you find him? when Mabry, his second son, came in the door.

SIXTEEN

EACH OF US IN TURN CLASPED DA CLOSE. HE TREMBLED, AS IF HE HAD A PALSY.

"'TIS HIS OWN SPIRIT COMING BACK," ANADEL SAID. "IT will need soothing."

She put the kettle on.

My mind was a hive of questions.

"Don't be troubling him with the how and why of things," she said to me. "That will come." And to Lily, she said, "Cut us the last of the old loaf, lass. Da must be famished."

He took only sips and crumbs, though, when we were all at table. He called our names and stroked our heads, our hands. He seemed older, our Da, almost an old man now, as if Bear, leaving, took years of his life.

"Will you not eat, Da?" Lily asked, offering him a bite of honeyed bread.

He took it. With the grain and nectar on his tongue, he closed his eyes. For a minute I feared he was lost again, but then he spoke. "Now it is over," he said.

"What, Da?" Lily asked. "What is over?"

And he said, "Do you remember your mother, Lily?"

She shook her head. Her gold curls gleamed in the firelight.

"Do you, Jamie?"

I tried hard. "Her voice," I said. "I remember that. And the song she sang."

"What song?" Ana wanted to know.

I hummed a minute, at first not getting it right. Then it came to me, and I sang:

> *"Shul, Shul, Shularoon*
> *Tree of sun and tree of moon*
> *Tree of root and tree of star*
> *'Tis dark and the journey far."*

"I wanted to find that tree," I told them.

"Aye," Da said, then went on. "Anadel, do you remember her?"

"I remember she was sick in winter," Ana said. "That was when I learned to keep the fire. I was afraid she might die, but you said, no, spring would heal her."

"And it always did, didn't it?" Da coaxed.

"Yes, Da," Ana answered.

I thought of bears, deep in dens, dreaming their way to spring.

Ana looked at me, then at Lily. "Why, she was in bed a long time before either of you were born."

"Was she a bear, then?" I asked.

"Our Ma?" Ana asked. "Was it our Ma in the cave?" And she began to cry.

"'Tis all right, Ana," Da said. "Let me tell you now." He poured tea in each of our cups. And on each of our plates put a bit of bread.

"Long ago and before long ago," he said, "some people grew tired of living in shelters and going out to hunt. They thought it would be easier to live in the forest, where food was plentiful. So they asked the Fur Men if they could come and live among them.

"'Yes,' said Bear. 'But once you join us, you cannot go back.'

"'Why would we want to return?' they said. 'Our life is hard labor. But you, you do not struggle all winter to get food and keep fire. You grow fat and sleep.'

"Bear scoffed at the foolishness of humans who did not know his driven days hunting in summer or fall, or reckon in lean years, the many who never woke.

"But Bear said, 'Welcome.'

"And the people grew fur and claws and slept the long sleep. But this they found much harder than the life they had known.

"And sometimes there was one among them who could not stay, one who longed for firelight and cradles and human talk. Given human food, such a one could shed the Bear form, though not Bear's whole nature. Given love, such a one could sustain the change for a time. But this was forbidden. This the first Bear-folk had promised not to do.

"Your mother was such a one. She watched me hunting in the woods and felt a great longing. And so, one summer's day as I lay dozing, she ate the bread I had brought and fell asleep by my side.

"Later, we both woke and marveled. She told me her plight, but I could not believe her. She was my dream of a heart's companion come true. How could she, slim and fair, belong to Bear? And if she did, then surely the ceremony, the golden ring of words, which bound her to me would free her from that hold.

"But it did not. Though she stayed with me all she could and bore you each, the day came when she had to go back. And her kin wanted you, too."

We looked at each other. "Wanted us to live with bears?" I asked.

Da nodded. "They claimed you as her cubs. Only if I submitted to a spell, laboring for them as a bear by day—white, so all would know me—could I keep you safe. But that protection was broken if another human entered their woods."

"So you forbade me—"

"Yes, son. Once you crossed that stream, our door was open to them."

"That is how Bear got me," Ana put in.

"Yes. And I would have gotten Lily, as well, if she were not so quick and nimble." Da smiled at Lily in his old way, and it did my heart good.

"You were the bear that took me? You?" Ana asked. Pain and confusion twisted her voice.

"I put you with your mother for the long sleep," Da said. "It was the only way to keep you safe."

"But you would have come back for *me*, wouldn't you, Da?" Lily asked.

Da drew Lily to him. "My Lily, I would have climbed the rafters after you."

We sat in silence for a while. Then Anadel, her voice easy again, asked, "But what broke the spell, Da?"

"It was this one," he said, putting his hand on my head. "'Twas you, Jamie, following me all the way to the Yew Tree, calling me, claiming me, though I stood as Bear before you. I tried to enchant you, to keep you safe in the tree, sleeping like a bear, but you would not have it and came after me again. You would have the world whole or not at all.

"And something told me to put you on the tree, that Ash Tree your ma sang about, that grows forever, connecting earth and sky. I did not know that once you were bound, I would be free."

"Then what freed Jamie?" Lily asked.

I looked at the ring on my finger, shimmering in the firelight. "A girl climbed the tree and cut me down," I said. "She breathed life into me and took me to the rockhouse."

"A *girl?*" Anadel said. "No girl would enter those woods. You must have dreamed that, Jamie. 'Twas shocked and frozen you were."

"But he has her ring," Lily insisted.

"'Tis your ma's ring," Da said. "The one I gave her."

"And it got your voice back, Da," Lily said, excited.

He looked at each of us in the circle. "Many mysteries," he said. "Many questions. But sleep is the answer we need now."

~ 17 ~

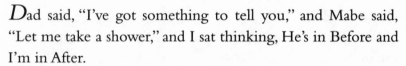

Dad said, "I've got something to tell you," and Mabe said, "Let me take a shower," and I sat thinking, He's in Before and I'm in After.

"Okay," Dad said. "But hurry it up."

Mabry looked at us then. It was like a little hook had snagged his attention before he went out of the room. "How was your trip with Taka?" he asked, eyebrows raised to indicate another question.

"Amazing," I told him, trying to answer it.

"Be right back," he said.

I couldn't just sit there. "I'll make some hot chocolate," I said, and got up from the table.

Cocoa, sugar, milk, vanilla, six or seven grains of salt . . . Martin, Jewel, Meg . . . everything was going around in my mind. . . . Kit, Mabry, Gina . . . Esther, the boy, the rockhouse . . . all of it stirred up—bitter, sweet . . . Mom not here anymore, not singing . . . Kit who never was here.

"In case you're wondering, I didn't find him," Dad said. He

stood, facing the bay window by the kitchen table. He looked out into the dark.

"Why not?" I asked, then thought, What a dumb question. Why *would* he find him? A boy was smashed on the road. What was there to find? Where?

"Esther says maybe he's not ready," Dad explained. "Maybe he is caught in his own trauma and can't deal with mine." Dad laughed. I mean, *laughed*.

I turned to him. "What's funny?"

"It would seem that people go on being people, even when they're dead."

This was really strange. The marshmallows were not in their cabinet.

"Caught up in their own stuff," Dad went on. "Bad timing."

"Caught up?" I echoed. The words sent chills down my back.

Dad went over to the pantry. He found a bag of miniature marshmallows and tossed them onto the counter. "Here you go," he said.

And the phone rang. I was so startled that I picked it up without thinking. Dad pointed at the answering machine, but it was too late.

"Hello," I said.

"Gina?" It was a voice I almost recognized. "Gina, it's Andrew."

"Andrew?" I couldn't believe it.

Now it was his turn to be surprised. "Didn't you call?" he asked.

"Yeah, but I forgot to leave my name."

He laughed. "My mom has this Caller ID thing. Tells the number and the name it's listed under—"

"I see." What I saw was Mabry coming down the stairs. "Listen, Andrew, I'd love to talk, but I can't right now. We're having sort of a . . . a family meeting."

"Hey, that's okay!" he said. "See you tomorrow?"

"Sure!" I told him. "Tomorrow." And hung up.

Dad had poured the hot chocolate, and Mabry, in clean sweats and smelling of herbal shampoo, took a seat at the table, saying, "So what's up?"

He looked from me to Dad and back again. Then he saw the steaming mugs on the table. Red mugs Mom had gotten us years ago for Valentine's Day. TAKE HEART is spelled out in flowers and arrows. "Mmmmmm," Mabry said, and licked his lips.

As soon as Dad and I sat down, Mabry glanced at me. I was stirring marshmallows into my hot chocolate, thinking about swirling snow.

"So where's your ring?" Mabry asked.

Who would have thought he'd notice?

"I lost it," I told him.

"I thought you couldn't get it off."

"What ring?" Dad asked.

"The one that came from Grandma Pierce," I said.

"How did you lose it if you couldn't get it off?" Mabry asked.

"I don't *know*," I said, exasperated. I handed him the clipping.

After a minute, he said, "Who's this?" and Dad began his confession again.

About three minutes into it, Mabry hit his forehead with the heel of his hand. "Dad!" he exclaimed. "That kid called here!"

"Kit?" Dad said, with sudden joy, as if somehow Kit might still be on the line. "When? When did he call?"

"I don't know—years ago," Mabry said. He had marshmallow on his upper lip.

"Think *hard,*" Dad urged.

"Well, Mom was in the driveway honking the horn because I had a baseball game and I was late because I was missing a sock, but I found it at the last minute on my lamp shade—"

"Mabry!" Dad said, leaning forward impatiently. "I don't care about your socks!"

"But if I could remember . . . hey, yeah! It was orange, so I was on the Orioles, and if I was on the Orioles, it was—"

"Why didn't you tell me?" Dad cut in.

"Fourth grade," Mabry finished. "I thought he was nuts. He calls up and asks to speak to you. I say you're not here but can I tell you who called. And he says, 'His son.' And I say, 'No, *I'm* his son.' And he says, 'Well, you're not the one and only.' I'm sure it's a prank, but I still ask if he wants to leave a message, and he says, 'No, thanks. Someday I may just show up at his door.'"

SEVENTEEN

DARKNESS CAME, AND DA
BEDDED US DOWN AS IF WE WERE BABIES, STROKING OUR
HAIR, TUCKING THE COVERS IN.

Wind was howling, but we were warm, the fire banked for
the night, Da's voice glowing:

> "An earthly nurse sits and sings,
> And aye, she sings by lily wean,
> And little ken I my bairn's father
> Far less the land where he dwells in.
>
> "I am a man upon the land,
> I am a silkie on the sea,
> And when I'm far and far frae land
> My home it is in Sule Skerrie."

'Tis a sad song, but we are not sad. We sleep on sweet leaves,
the husk of love about us. And it is our own Da who sings, our
own Da, who will be with us still come morning.

~ 18 ~

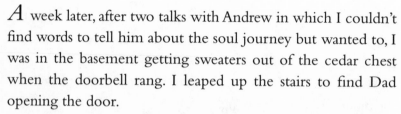

A week later, after two talks with Andrew in which I couldn't find words to tell him about the soul journey but wanted to, I was in the basement getting sweaters out of the cedar chest when the doorbell rang. I leaped up the stairs to find Dad opening the door.

A round girl, not much older than Mabry, and a skinny little boy, both in jeans and T-shirts, stood on the porch. Her black hair was close-cut except for a thin, beaded braid that hung over one eye. The kid's pale hair was longer than hers and he wore little hiking boots.

"Hi," she said, like we'd been introduced.

"May I help you?" Dad asked.

She let go of the little boy's hand and touched his shoulders. He scooted around in front of her. "You're Dr. Ourisman, right?" she asked.

Dad nodded.

"It's about him," she said.

It was cold, and the boy's shirt was thin. "Why don't you come in?" I said, then glanced at Dad.

"Yes, please," he said.

I thought she must need a doctor for her little boy. Maybe she didn't know Dad was a surgeon.

He showed them into the family room, and we all sat down, the girl in the green leather rocker, the boy on the footstool.

"How may I help you?" Dad asked again.

"Kit McFerran is your son, right?" the girl asked.

Dad's doctor-look vanished. "He was."

"Well, I'm Halley Neal, Kit's girlfriend, and he came to me last night in a dream. I was all excited, ready for a message, because *I* loved him, and we never said good-bye. He hit that tree and he was gone. But what he said was, 'Tell him, Halley. Promise.' I woke up mad, but I had to do what he said, so I got your address from Jewel and here I am."

"Tell me what?" Dad asked, his voice husky.

The girl lifted her chin, tightened her mouth. "That we had this boy," she said.

Silence. Halley watched our faces. The little boy looked at his boots.

"What's his name?" I asked.

"Christopher James," she said. "After Kit."

Christopher James looked up. "I'm Jamie," he said.

Dad was pretty good with this whole thing, really. He welcomed the two of them, looked at pictures of Kit, sent out for pizza—something we never do—and generally gave Halley and Jamie the day. He even tried to talk to Jamie, but he didn't get very far.

Mabe, on the other hand, Mabe who never even notices kids—there could be redheaded triplet babies at the table and he'd just reach around them for the ketchup—Mabe hit it off with Jamie immediately. "You like LEGOs?" he asked.

Jamie nodded.

"Star Wars?"

"Yes!"

"Then hold on," Mabry told him. And he produced out of his bedroom closet two big plastic tubs full of plastic blocks and people, creatures, spaceships, and weapons. And he sat down on the floor in the family room with Jamie to play.

Halley just watched them. I invited her to come see the kitchen or come upstairs to my room, but she didn't budge. Maybe it was because she wasn't a kid *or* a grown-up. Or maybe she was afraid if she wasn't watching, we'd grab Jamie and run off with him.

So I sat there watching too. Dad brought in juice, then went to order the pizza. When he asked Halley what they liked on it, she just said, "Whatever," so we got cheese.

Jamie was building what he called a "realator"—a sort of gun that could "put the real in or take it away" from whatever you shot with it—when Mabry said, "I guess your dad and I were brothers."

"I guess," Jamie said, not looking up from his creation.

"So I'm your uncle," Mabry went on.

"Um-hmm," Jamie said, still not looking up.

"And I'm your aunt," I put in.

Dad walked into the room just then. "Do you remember your dad?" he asked.

Jamie shook his head.

"So we're kind of alike," Dad said, squatting down by his grandson. "He was my son, and I didn't know him either."

Jamie showed no response to this, but Halley said, "Yeah, but you had a choice."

"Fair enough," Dad responded.

Finally, the doorbell rang, bringing two boxes of Domino's finest.

We sat around the kitchen table, crowded like it used to be when Mom was there and Mabe or I had a friend over, working at conversation while Jamie peeled the cheese off two slices of pizza and ate it like a bird eats a worm.

"I just like the bark," he said.

We all laughed, but then I caught sight of my hand on the white table and the knife by my plate, and for some reason, the room seemed to turn over backward. "Whoa!" I said, holding on to the table.

"What's up?" Mabry asked.

"I just got dizzy all of a sudden."

"Lean over and put your head between your knees," Dad advised.

"No, I'm okay," I said. "It's gone now."

And the dizziness *was* gone. I just felt weird around the edges, like when you almost remember something.

We finished eating, and Dad offered to take Halley and Jamie home.

"It's all right," Halley said. "I got Jewel's car."

So she gave Dad her address and phone number, and he

offered her some money, which at first she wouldn't take but then she did, and they disappeared out the door.

"That was weird," Mabry said as soon as the latch clicked.

Dad didn't comment but headed straight to the kitchen to clean up.

And I remembered my hand and the knife, the world falling. It was the frozen bark, my hand stabbing the tree. "Depends on your weirdness scale," I said, and went out to help Dad.

As I was putting Jamie's pizza crusts in the disposal, I said, "Dad, I think we need to see Esther again."

To my amazement, he replied, "My thought exactly."

That night when we sat around with the television on— another thing we hardly ever do—Dad told Mabry about Esther and asked if he'd like to come with us, but Mabry said absolutely not.

"It's enough to find out I have a brother only after he's dead, and I've been an uncle since before I could shave. I don't need to throw in a talk with Mom's psycho-healer."

"Psychic, not psycho," Dad told him. "If you don't want to come, that's fine. Scorn is not necessary."

Mabry shrugged his shoulders. "Sorry," he said. And then, "I guess."

Dad didn't follow up on this remark the way he would have before, pursuing till he got the last word. Instead, he reached over to Mabry on the couch and gave him a little shove. Like guys do! I couldn't believe it. Mabe looked at Dad and then at me and smiled. It was a moment.

I said if Mabry wasn't coming, could we take Taka, but Dad said no, this was just for family. I started to protest that Taka sort of *was* family, and that she was already involved, but with Halley and Jamie in it now, I could see what he meant.

Anyway, Tuesday was Esther's day off, and somehow Dad left work early and picked me up after school. As we drove out of the city, I told him about the soul journey with Esther, and how I remembered it at the table when Halley and Jamie were there. "Do you think there's a connection?" I asked.

"Between what?" he asked.

"Between my journey and them showing up?"

"No," Dad said. "How could there be?"

"I don't know," I said, confused. "It just feels like it, that's all."

We drove along in silence, then, till we turned off at the Akron exit and I said, "Why does Esther work at McDonald's, anyway?"

"Did you see cars waiting in line at her house?" Dad asked.

"No," I said.

"You'll find a lot more people want Big Macs than want soul journeys."

"I know that," I said. "But couldn't she do something more related?"

"I think she wants the contrast," Dad said. "I imagine it keeps her grounded, being in touch with all kinds of people every day."

"Grounded and greasy," I said. Dad laughed. He was different since Halley had showed up. More there.

✳

It wasn't even five o'clock when we got to Esther's but, being November, it was already getting dark. Wind rattled the last leaves on the trees, and the empty fields around her house looked sad.

But the house was warm and bright.

"Gina, Martin, come in!" Esther said. "I can't believe you are here together!" And she led us through ordinary rooms to her kitchen, alive with color. As soon as I saw the rosy table, half of me said, Yes! And the other half wanted to run out the door.

"We're just going to talk, right?" I asked as we sat down. The teakettle began its high whistle.

Esther turned the burner down. "I don't know, Gina," she answered. "I guess I'll see what you need. Is peppermint tea good, or would you like orange?"

"Orange," we both said at once.

So we sat at the table, the blue teapot between us. There was a honey dish as well as sugar and milk set out, and I put honey in my mug before Esther even poured the tea. I liked to look at its golden weight, to think of all the flowers whose nectar was stored there, to think of wings and work and summer. . . . I shook my head.

"What is it, Gina?" Esther asked. She looked older to me this time. Maybe it was the purple flannel shirt. It didn't exactly go with red hair.

"I've only been here ten minutes," I told her, "and already I'm thinking weird stuff."

Esther laughed. "Like what?"

So I told her about the honey, and she said, "You're just see-ing connections. That's not weird. That's great."

"But I'm not trying to," I protested. "Are you"—I hesitated at this point, but then went on, feeling I had to ask—"are you doing something to my mind?"

"Gina!" Dad said. He sounded embarrassed.

"No, it's a good question," Esther said. "It can be done, and you're wise to be wary. But I would never do that, Gina. Not with you, not with anyone." She reached over and patted my hand. "I think your consciousness is just more open here, remembering your other visit."

"Dad told you about Halley and Jamie?" I asked.

Esther poured the tea, one freckled hand keeping the lid on the teapot. "Yes," she said. "I think it's wonderful."

"Well—?" I couldn't get myself to ask the question.

Silence. The clock ticked. A stitch in time, I thought. Tick, tock. Clock hands like needles. Dad sipped his tea. Finally he said, "I think what we want to know is, is there a connection between what Gina did here and Halley's coming to see us?"

"Do you feel there is?" Esther asked.

"Of course!" I blurted out. "I can't help it."

"Well, there's your answer," she replied.

"But *what?*" I asked. "It doesn't make any sense."

"Oh, but it does," Esther said. "Just not the kind you're used to."

"So tell me what kind," I insisted.

"Try your tea," she said. I did. The honey was delicious, sweet as, sweet as . . .

"Bears!" I said.

"What?" Dad asked.

"It has something to do with bears."

"Halley and Jamie?" Dad sounded confused.

"No, no. Where I went. Where I found the boy."

"Did you see bears?" Esther asked.

I shook my head. "I just know," I said. "Only—" My voice caught. I had to get a hold of myself. I didn't want—

"Will won't work," Esther said.

Now *I* was the one left behind. "What?" I asked her.

"Will won't lead you, won't teach you what you need to know."

"That's creepy!" I almost shouted. "You *did* get in my head!"

"Gina," Esther said, reaching over to take my hands in hers, "there are many ways of knowing. Your pain is not so hidden . . ."

I pulled my hands away. "So tell me about the bears."

"I don't know," Esther said. "Do you want to go back and see?"

"No!"

Dad started to speak, but Esther held up her hand to signal Wait.

"Just tell me what the boy on the tree had to do with Halley bringing Jamie. Then we can go home."

"I'm afraid I can't provide the kind of explanation you want," Esther said. "This is not like a math problem."

"I tell people that same thing," Dad offered. "In the body, things happen. Medical science doesn't always know why."

"But it's deeper than that," Esther told him, then turned her attention to me. She took a spoonful of tea from her cup. "What would you see, Gina, if you put some of this on a slide and looked at it through a microscope?"

"Lots of stuff," I said. "There could be germs, dust particles, bits of tea leaves . . ."

"And is it there now?" she asked. "Though you can't see it?"

"Sure," I told her.

"It's like a whole other world, right?"

I nodded.

"And does this other world affect us?" Esther asked.

"Of course."

"Did it affect us before we knew it was there?"

"Yes."

"Well, think of the place you went on your soul journey as like that invisible world."

"Or like the one hidden inside it," Dad said, warming to the topic. "With better microscopes, we could see inside the germ, too."

"Exactly," Esther said. "And so it goes—"

"On down to subatomic particles," Dad interjected.

Esther laughed. "Those I don't know about."

"I know a little," I said, "because Taka's taking physics."

"So what do you know?" Dad asked.

"Taka says the particles communicate somehow, but it doesn't make sense that they can."

"That's *right!*" Dad said excitedly. "The way they communicate defies space and time."

"There you have it," said Esther.

"But I'm not some quark!" I declared, frustrated with all this discussion. "I *saw* things. I felt them. I went somewhere!"

"I know that," she said.

I was starting to shake now, like there was ice down my back and the cold was working its way to my hands and head and feet.

"There now, Gina," Dad said, patting me on the back. Esther got up and took an afghan from the couch and put it over my shoulders.

"*This* reality," Esther began, coming back to her place at the table, "this room with this table and us around it, this is only one layer, Gina. Pushed by concern for your father and guided by a longing of your own, you slipped out of this layer very easily. That openness is one of your mother's gifts to you. And when you slipped out, where you found your-self somehow connects—I don't know how—with your story. We can only wonder at it. Wonder is our way of understanding."

"But the boy on the tree—" Dad said, his voice intense. "Kit was killed by hitting a tree."

"I know," Esther said.

"And in this other world I got a boy down from a tree, got him warm, and took him to the rockhouse."

"Yes," Esther said.

"And when I got the fire going I fell asleep beside him. I knew we were all right, that we wouldn't die. But I didn't dream—"

"Halley dreamed," Dad cut in. "And Kit spoke to her." His voice was full of feeling. "It's like you cut *him* free, Gina, to send us Jamie. When I tried, he wouldn't talk to me, but through you, he gave me another chance."

"Is that it?" I asked Esther.

"That seems to be part of it," she said, handing Dad a Kleenex. "This is hard work. I think we need some food."

While Esther was putting pita bread in a basket and setting out something to spread on it, I looked at my dad. None of his patients would recognize this man. Oh, he was dressed the same: everything pressed and matched and fitting perfectly. But his face didn't fit anymore. It was an open face, hurt and broken. I wasn't the only one who'd been on a journey.

Esther sat back down and dealt us each a little plate, one yellow, one purple, one blue. She passed the breadbasket.

"So how is it only part?" I asked.

"Well," Esther said, "there's the other boy, the one whose life you saved. His story. You didn't make your journey just for this layer, for your reality. Something called you."

I pulled the afghan closer around me. It smelled like wood smoke and the big ginger cat who'd been curled up on it when we came. Like Mom and Whit's house in the mountains. I took a deep breath. I didn't have to say anything. I didn't have to go any farther.

"How much farther?" I had asked in the woods, hiking in August.

"Just till we get there," Whit had answered.

Suddenly my eyes were hot with tears. "I've been in those woods before!" I exclaimed.

"Where?" Dad asked.

"The place where I saved the boy. It was in a dream I had the night before I called you, Esther. It was Christmas— before the divorce—and you gave me a snow globe, Dad, a present you had tucked in the tree. And when I opened the package and turned the globe upside down, all at once I was *in* there, on that snowy path. So I *was* called—"

"Slow down, Gina. Slow down and let yourself breathe," Esther counseled. She took one of my hands, and Dad took the other. I closed my eyes.

I felt like I might just leave my body, like something deep inside was pressing me out. I was right at the border. I was sifted through a screen.

And I stood before a wooden door, a brown door in a cottage of round stones, a door with the moon and stars carved above it and a vine growing around it. The door opened, and there he stood, my boy, with his crow-black hair and his gray eyes. He was barefoot, wearing pants and a shirt of the rough brown cloth I remembered, but now his face was warm and his eyes bright and smiling. He held up his hand, palm outward, and I matched mine to it, feeling a jolt of heat and sweetness as they met. Grandma Pierce's ring was on his finger. Or was it *his* ring that she had worn, that Mom had given to me? Was this before or after?

From behind the boy a man's voice called, "Who is it, lad?"

"'Tis nobody, Da," the boy said, taking his hand back, but

still looking deep into my eyes. "Only the light dancing."

There was no mother in that house. Somehow I knew it. But a young woman's voice said, "Dancing light—go on with you!"

A little girl, almost giggling, added, "Aye, he's daft, our Jamie." And he closed the door.

I opened my eyes and saw Dad and Esther at the kitchen table still holding my hands.

"What happened?" Dad asked.

I knew then what stone and trees and birds know, what the waterfall spills and spells. All was well. But I didn't have any words. Only the print of Jamie's hand in mine. Only the light dancing.